I
KNOW
YOU
LIED

BOOKS BY LESLEY SANDERSON

The Orchid Girls
The Woman at 46 Heath Street
The Leaving Party

I
KNOW
YOU
LIED

LESLEY SANDERSON

bookouture

Published by Bookouture in 2020

An imprint of Storyfire Ltd.
Carmelite House
50 Victoria Embankment
London EC4Y 0DZ

www.bookouture.com

ISBN: 978-1-83888-112-2
eBook ISBN: 978-1-83888-111-5

To Uncle Rob and Aunty Pat, with love

PROLOGUE

It has finally happened.

The letter arrived on Friday the thirteenth. Not usually a significant date for me – I'm not one of those people who pander to superstitious nonsense – but afterwards, when I had calmed down, it made me pause a moment and wonder.

It arrived when I was preparing my morning coffee. Strong, with a dash of cream, just how I like it. My cleaner never did get it quite right, despite so many years of practice. The rattle of the letter box alerted me and I could hear the postman whistling as he walked away from the house. Pain spread through my bones as I bent down to retrieve the letter from the bristly doormat. Did I suspect then that it had happened, the unravelling of events that I had dreaded for years?

The envelope was the beige of letters of import – a bank statement, perhaps, or a bill – but when I turned it over to reveal the familiar name of the solicitors' firm, unease stirred inside me.

I took a sip of coffee and opened the letter. When I saw the subject matter, I let the scalding liquid run down my throat. I imagined it making its way through my body as the implications of what her death would mean trickled into my mind. No doubt Nell would be reading it too. It would be too much to expect that she wouldn't be contacted. How could I stop this?

I'd heard that my solicitor had been trying to get in touch with me but had never anticipated this. Over the years it had occurred to me as a possibility, a fleeting one, but I'd trained myself never to allow my thoughts to go in that direction. Think positive, I'd told myself, as I'd told others so many times.

She'd been found in her flat in London, the cause of death as yet to be determined. She was in her fifties, far too young to die, but she'd had a hard life, which was entirely her own doing. Now old secrets that had been so deeply buried would rise to the surface and spill forth, and I had to be prepared to put a stop to it. Whatever it took. I didn't doubt my capability of resorting to extreme measures, though; after all, I'd already done the worst. What did I have to lose?

CHAPTER ONE

2019

It all begins with the letter from the solicitor. Thick beige envelope, expensive, the name of the firm printed on the back: Grayling and Hurst, Solicitors. Nell is mildly curious but leaves it on the table for now, relieved to finally kick off her shoes and enjoy her evening. Takeaway pizza, she'd decided. It's been a long day, after all, and colder weather is setting in. Melted cheese and a bit of stodge is exactly the comfort food she needs.

It was one of those ordinary days at work, rushing around as she does every day of her life, phone stuck to her ear and inbox bursting with unread emails, trying to get more done than the allotted time would allow and ending the day with her head feeling like it was encased in a too-tight helmet. She enjoys working as an events manager but deep down is starting to wish she could find a less intense career in which to express her creative side.

The innocent remark made by her boss, Stacey, last week – that she should take some leave and go back to the coastal village she grew up in – caught her unawares. Stacey was oohing and aahing about how lovely that must have been and wondering how on earth she ended up in the city. Nell recalls the way her body stiffened. That particular nugget she keeps to herself. She doesn't go down that route for anyone. She looks around the flat, which is all hers – the walls she lovingly repainted in a cool grey last year, the few but much-coveted items of furniture she's worked so hard to save for – and smiles to herself. Her life in London, which she's built from scratch, is what matters now. Her phone buzzes and she knows it will be Hannah, excited about their night out this weekend: a film followed by a meal, where they can pull the movie apart and talk about their week.

She puts the kettle on, sticks a tea bag in her favourite chipped mug and wonders about the solicitor's letter. She's pretty confident she hasn't committed any crimes lately. The one parking ticket she's received – wrongly in her opinion, but it wasn't worth the hassle of contesting it – was paid immediately. Her life is like this: a series of imagined scenarios she creates for herself every night before she goes to sleep – alone in her king-size bed since her recent split with Sam – and which mostly bear no relation to what is really happening in her life. Like winning an award for her fantastic flute playing when she's never even picked up the instrument. A girl can dream, can't she? A close family would be her wish of choice, as simple and as complicated as that. The less she thinks about her family, the better.

Wrapping her hands around the mug, she goes back to the letter she's discarded on the sofa, willing it to contain something exciting. She tries to recall the last time she received a letter that wasn't a bill. Lilian used to tell her of a time when people wrote letters to their friends – long, handwritten, lovingly crafted letters, which, once sent on their way, meant an agonising wait for the postman. Lilian. Her grandmother. She tries not to think about her often, but it's too late: she's looming in Nell's head and her stomach turns over, as if steeling itself for an indigestible meal.

She straightens her back, shoulders down, takes deep breaths and reminds herself who she is, how far she has come.

When Nell last saw her grandmother, she had a mane of tight silver curls, a cloud of steel wool around her head. Nell has that thick hair too, but hers is blonde, with a distinctive silver streak at the front, and her curls are loose, created with a clever implement. Lilian never had time for such frippery.

The mug of tea burns her fingertips and she can't put it down fast enough. She opens the letter and slides out the contents: one sheet of paper with a gold crest at the top and a single paragraph of writing.

Dear Ms Wetherby,

You are requested to attend the offices of Grayling and Hurst on Friday 4 October at 11 a.m. to discuss the will of Sarah Wetherby, of which you are a beneficiary.

    Please confirm that you will be attending.

Yours sincerely,
Jonathan Grayling, solicitor

The news hits Nell as if she's been shot, and she's on her feet, breathing hard, knocking the table, which causes tea to spill over her hand. The letter has to be some kind of prank, but who could be so cruel? She reads it through again, and again, but the words are there in black and white: not many of them, but their impact is no less powerful. Her thoughts are racing. What if it's not a prank? Could it be true? She sits down, then jumps up again as if a puppet master is pulling her strings. Is this the work of her grandmother? Lilian has always made her feel like that, that she must dance to her disagreeable tune. That's the reason she left home at sixteen.

Rational thought returns. She locates her phone and squints at the address and phone number at the top of the letter. An SW3 postcode, Chelsea: upmarket, very Lilian if she's right about this having something to do with her grandmother. The name is familiar – yes, she's convinced these are her grandmother's solicitors too. She keys in the number.

As she listens to the dial tone, she becomes aware of her hand smarting where she scalded it with tea. Pushing back her sleeve to see how bad it is, she can't help glimpsing the unsightly mark that has plagued her all her life, deep red and ugly. The mark Grandma said she was born with, though a nurse once told her otherwise. But Grandma was always right and the nurse was young, inexperienced.

She focuses on her tea to calm herself, blows hard to cool it down, a ball of anxiety in her throat. But the woman who answers is softly spoken and kind as she puts her through to Mr Grayling, who explains that yes, indeed, as stated in the letter, she is named in the will of Sarah Wetherby – her mother, he believes – and will she be attending, and Ms Wetherby, are you OK?

Nell is not OK, far from it; how could she ever be OK again, because this person can't possibly be her mother. Her mother died in an accident when Nell was a baby. This woman has to be an impostor. But the cold finger of fear presses against her heart. If this is true, her grandmother has lied to her her whole life. Why would she behave so cruelly?

She sits for ages as the light dims around her and night falls outside, the words going round and round in her head. When she finally managed to speak and stop the solicitor from hanging up, convinced either that he was dealing with an imbecile or that the line had gone dead, she swallowed the boulder in her throat and asked him to tell her what had happened to her mother.

Sarah Wetherby had died alone, impoverished and under-nourished, in the one-bedroom flat she'd lived in since her arrival in London twenty-six years ago. Nell sank to the floor then and listened, trying not to let her pain spill out. She wanted to wail and sob and rage but held it all inside her like a tight ball of string.

'Are you all right?' Mr Grayling asked, and part of her wanted to let the truth pour out, but it was too improbable a tale to tell and in that moment she could scarcely believe it herself.

When the solicitor was no longer on the phone and had gone back to his day, which was much the same as any other day of his life, Nell went back to hers, which is forever changed. Her gut tells her this is her mother. A cold hand squeezes her heart. Her mother has been living in the same city as her this whole time, desperate for help, and Nell had no idea. Did she know her daughter was here? Or was the truth kept from her too? Why did she never try and find Nell, and why did she leave in the first place?

The tea is cold when she comes back to life, lifting her head and gazing into the murky brown liquid. She goes out onto her balcony and inhales the cold evening air. It revives her, and anger burns through her. Pigeons gather on the adjacent rooftops, heads bobbing as they scavenge for food. Nell's eyes scan the London skyline. The answers aren't to be found there, or anywhere else in this sprawling city. The answers lie back in Seahurst, and she knows who holds them. Her grandmother. It is Lilian Wetherby who has done this to her.

She closes the balcony door behind her, shivering, and reads through the letter once more. The meeting is tomorrow morning. She's too emotional to call her manager and sends her a text instead. Thankfully tomorrow is Friday, which means she'll have the head space to get herself together over the weekend. Already stress is mounting up as she does a mental run-through of all the tasks she'd planned to do tomorrow. Ironic that only hours earlier she was thinking of all that leave she should be taking, but working as an events manager means there is always a project on the go, so it's hard to leave things behind, and she never trusts anyone to do things as well as she would. If nothing else, her grandmother taught her to be self-sufficient.

She spends an hour cancelling appointments and dealing with urgent emails, and it keeps her focused. Tomorrow she will write a new list. But as the evening draws on and her eyes grow heavy, the night ahead looms like an ominous shadow. Business concluded, she pours herself a large glass of red wine, puts some music on and thinks about her mother, this woman who up until today she knew nothing about.

CHAPTER TWO

'You must be Ms Wetherby.' The tall man in an immaculate grey suit steps out from behind his desk to shake her hand. Thick dark hair peppered with grey and expressive eyebrows over blue eyes. He's around fifty, his handshake is firm and Nell senses she is in capable hands. Her anxiety lessens slightly. 'Jonathan Grayling. Welcome to Grayling and Hurst. May I get you tea, coffee, a glass of water?'

'Water, please,' she says. 'And please, call me Nell.'

She has spent the last hour sitting in the café across the road, a bitter cup of coffee growing cold in front of her. She's made a note of all the questions she needs to ask. She wonders whether anyone else will be attending, is preparing herself just in case.

Mr Grayling slides a coffee pod into a sleek-looking Nespresso machine and Nell tries to relax, inhaling the smell of coffee that permeates the room. His offices are in an old building and his room is large and airy, with big windows looking out over a park. His desk is neat and polished, with one of those executive toys where you flick a ball to make the others move. A terrible urge to tap it overtakes Nell and she holds the water glass tight to stop herself from reacting inappropriately.

Jonathan Grayling takes a file from his in tray and opens it. 'The last will and testament of Sarah Wetherby.' He looks over his glasses at her.

'Are you expecting anyone else?' She holds her breath as she waits for his answer.

'No,' he says. 'Before we start…' He takes off his glasses, and his eyes are kind. 'Obviously I know a little about this case, being your grandmother's solicitor. Had you been estranged from your mother for a long time?'

Nell gazes out of the window, her smile ironic. 'You could say that. I was told when I was young that my mother died in a car accident.'

'Goodness,' he says. 'Who told you that – if you don't mind talking about it, that is?'

'No, it's a relief really. My grandmother brought me up.'

'That would be…' He refers to his notes. 'Lilian Wetherby. She was down as Sarah's next of kin. I tried to contact her but she didn't respond to my letter.'

'We're estranged. Not completely; we have minimum contact where necessary.'

Memories of the last contact floods into her head. The obligatory Christmas card, one word inside – Lilian – a word with a thousand meanings. 'I left home when I was sixteen and moved to London. My grandmother smothered me. We lived in Seahurst, a small seaside town in Sussex, and I'd been desperate to break free for most of my life. Living with one other person was hard. Lilian didn't drive, and the bus service was so unreliable, and none of my friends lived nearby.' Most of the time Lilian had wanted to keep Nell tethered to her. She'd been like a dog tied to a post, straining at the leash yet unable to escape.

'And presumably she was the one who told you your mother had died. Are there any other relatives?'

'She had a sister, but I never met her. They didn't communicate. Lilian was – is – a difficult woman.'

'I understand. This must have been rather a shock to you, I imagine. I'm sorry it's been difficult. Hopefully it will at least bring you closer to your late mother.'

He pulls the folder towards him.

'We might as well make a start. It shouldn't take long, as you are the only beneficiary. I've made a copy for you to look at.' He passes a piece of A4 paper across the desk, his hand steady. Nell feels anything but. 'If I may direct you to the relevant clause: paragraph three – "I, Sarah Wetherby, being of sound mind and disposing memory, do hereby give my entire estate to my daughter Eleanor Mary Wetherby."'

Nell follows the words through blurry eyes. Some legal jargon follows, before the solicitor says, 'She makes particular reference to a gold locket necklace she would like you to have. I'll be honest,' he goes on, 'there is little of any financial value to inherit. She was renting her property and had no savings. I'm afraid to say she died in somewhat impoverished circumstances. However, I believe the gift of the necklace will be of immense emotional value to you. I have it here.'

He takes a small package from his drawer. Nell's fingers tremble as she opens the box, in which lies a gold locket on a chain. Her fingers fumble at the clasp. Her head feels light; she wonders whether there will be a photo inside.

'Allow me.' Mr Grayling gets to his feet and takes the delicate necklace from her. He gently opens the locket with his long fingers. 'There,' he says, 'a photograph on either side in the traditional fashion. Your mother and yourself, I believe.'

He passes it back to Nell and she peers at the two tiny photographs. A chubby-cheeked baby with huge serious eyes stares at the camera on one side, but it is the other that seizes her attention: the blonde woman with the heart-shaped face and the exact same eyes as Nell. Her gaze is direct, serious. A gasp escapes Nell's mouth, which she covers with her hands.

'I've never seen a photograph of my mother.' She raises her head to look at him, her eyes full of tears.

'Let me get you a cup of tea,' he says, and goes outside to speak to the receptionist. 'I have some other things for you here,' he says when he returns. 'The keys to her flat. I understand the landlord has allocated two weeks to clearing the place out, and I'm afraid that task will be left to you to organise. I can recommend a clearance company should you require advice. Will you be arranging the funeral?'

Nell swallows. 'I hadn't thought. I suppose I will.' Through the dark fog in her mind she remembers Hannah's dad. 'My best friend's father is a funeral director. I'll ask him to help me.'

'Excellent. That will no doubt be an enormous help in this difficult time.' He hands her an envelope. 'The address and keys and some other information you may require are in here.'

'Thanks.' The keys bulge in the envelope and Nell grips it in her palm.

Moments later, the receptionist comes in with a mug and a warm smile.

'Would you like to sit in our family room?' she asks Nell. 'It's a quiet area where you can take some time to think about your loss and what you've learned from us today. Most people find wills upsetting in some way.'

Nell nods. 'Thank you,' she says to Mr Grayling, and he shakes her hand.

'Any questions, here's my card.'

She follows the woman into a small room adjacent to the reception. It's a bit like how she imagines a therapist's room might look: small table, box of tissues, comfortable chair, a colourful print on the wall.

'I'm out here if you need anything,' the receptionist says. 'Take as long as you need.'

Once she's gone, Nell rips open the envelope. The address on the piece of paper makes her breath catch in her throat. It's so close to where she herself lives. If she'd known her mother was alive, would she have been able to find her? Would her mother have wanted to see her, or was Nell a shameful secret to be hidden away?

She opens a Google Earth search for the address and zooms in on the block where she thinks her mother lived. It's an ugly high-rise: flats with cluttered balconies, heavy-duty iron gates guarding the front doors. Imagining her dying here makes Nell feel unimaginably sad.

There isn't anything else in the envelope; most of her mother's possessions will be in her flat, which Nell will have to sort out. Another task she has to steel herself to face. She takes out the locket and gazes at the photos. She snaps a couple of shots with her phone, not wanting to risk losing the images. Lilian saw photos and mirrors as symbols of vanity, so there are few pictures of Nell as a child, but it's not her own photo she's interested in; it's the woman who shares her facial features and whose blood runs through her veins. She makes a promise to herself that she will do everything she can to find out what happened to her, and to know her story.

She finishes her tea and takes the mug out to reception.

'Could you fasten this locket for me?' she asks.

'It's pretty,' the woman says, taking the delicate chain and looping it around Nell's neck. It tickles where it falls. Nell presses the cold metal against her chest, feeling the beat of her heart underneath; unlike the beat of her mother's, which is forever silent. Tears well.

'Yes,' she says. 'It was my mother's.'

She splashes her face with cold water in the bathroom before she leaves, stares at her image, her eyes a little puffy, and scoops her hair back over her shoulders so that the necklace can be seen. As she does so, her sleeve slips up her arm, revealing the ugly mark she avoids looking at. Her mother would have known the truth about this, wouldn't she?

She makes a vow to herself: she will not rest until she gets answers to her questions. This will mean travelling back to Seahurst, confronting her grandmother and asking her why she told her such a cruel lie. Who was she trying to punish by keeping them apart?

What could her mother possibly have done to make Lilian hate her so much? Is her father really dead? Did the car accident he supposedly died in actually happen? Now she regrets her refusal to find out the details of the accident when she was younger, but at the time she couldn't face it, and her grandmother discouraged her from looking into it. 'The present is what counts' was one of her favourite sayings. She liked sayings. How does Nell know that any of the little she has been told about herself is true? Lilian guarded information like a state secret.

The first thing she does when she gets home is call Hannah. She almost calls Sam – instinct – but stops herself. That relationship belongs in the past, and it would be wrong to give him false hope when she just wants someone to hold her and make everything better.

'You still on for this weekend?' Hannah says without preamble.

'I'm sorry, Hannah. I can't make it.'

'Please don't do this to me, Nell! Tom is driving me mad at the moment and a girlie night out is just what I need. You'd better have a good reason. Are you missing Sam?'

'No, it's not that.' Nell sighs. 'I'd much rather be going out with you, but a family situation has come up.'

Hannah splutters. 'What family? Has a long-lost relative crawled out of the woodwork?'

'That's closer to the truth than you can possibly realise.' Nell sighs again. 'It's very complicated. I have to go back and see my grandmother.'

'Not the Big Bad Wolf?'

'Don't.' Hannah's name for Lilian usually makes her smile. She came up with it one night on a Greek island holiday when they'd overdone it on the ouzo and Nell had shared her story for the first time – only the bare bones of it, but enough for Hannah to coin the nickname and somehow make it easier to bear. 'It's the last thing I want to do, but I've got no choice.'

'Why? You're being very mysterious.'

'Her solicitor got in touch with me. I have to go back to Seahurst tomorrow.' She clears her throat and says the impossible words aloud. 'My mother has just died.'

'But…'

'Yes, I know. I thought she died when I was a baby. My grandmother lied to me.'

'Oh, Nell. That's awful. Do you know why?'

'I can't imagine, and that's why I'm going to Seahurst. I want to look Lilian in the eye and watch her face when I ask her what really happened.' She bursts into tears. 'She was in London, Han, all this time, and I didn't know.'

'I'm so sorry. Shall I come over? I can be there in half an hour.'

'No, I'll be all right. I need some time to get my head round this. I want to be on my own tonight, but I love you for offering. The solicitor asked me about the funeral, though…'

'Dad will sort it, that's something we can definitely help you with. Give me the solicitor's details and leave it to me. When you feel up to it, we can talk through the plans, or just put them in a text, if that's easier.'

'Thanks.'

'How long will you be gone for?'

'Not long, I hope. I'll keep you posted.'

Next she calls Stacey at work. She doesn't go into details; it's enough to say that her mother has died and she has some personal business to sort out that means travelling out of London. Stacey tells her she's entitled to a week of special leave in the first instance and then they can see how it goes. Nell feels relief when she's finished the conversation; work has burnt her out lately and she needs this enforced break.

She books her train tickets for the day after tomorrow; that way she'll have time to visit Sarah's flat first and see how much stuff there is to sort out. She makes a call to the landlord to let him know she'll be visiting. As she paces up and down, she catches sight of herself in the mirror. Once the call is finished, she opens the image she took of the photo in the locket and studies it, holds it up next to herself in front of the mirror, but the image is too small to make a proper comparison. She can't tell whether her mother had freckles across her nose too, and the same wide smile.

Up until today, the little she knew about her mother would have fitted on a postcard. Her name was Sarah Mary Wetherby and she died in a car accident, along with her husband, David. She was twenty-three years old and they had been married for barely three years. Once, aged about eight, when her classmates asked her about her mother, Nell took their questions home to her grandmother. Lilian closed down the conversation. Nell would only dare ask her about it one more time.

She strokes the locket, which is no longer cold, but warm against her breastbone, as she vows to turn the postcard into a letter and bring her mother back to life.

CHAPTER THREE

Nell stands in front of the high-rise block and checks her phone with a swooping feeling in her stomach. It's definitely the right address. Craning her neck, she looks up at the grey boxes stacked one on top of another and wonders which one was her mother's. She counts around fourteen storeys, does a quick calculation – say six flats on each level; even if only one or two people lived in each flat, there are easily over a hundred people who could have noticed the lonely woman and reached out to help her. She makes a mental note to increase the amount of money she sends to a charity for vulnerable people every month. Her mood has been low since she heard the news, and although grieving is natural, she wonders. So much is attributed to genetics these days; who knows what genes she has inherited from her mother?

A young boy stands in front of the entrance, holding a large twig. As she draws closer, she sees a cat, back arched and staring at him.

'Oi, pack it in,' she says, making the boy jump. The cat streaks past her and the boy turns and glares. Nell returns the glare and enters the tower block.

The lift isn't working, a tatty sign from the housing association stuck on the door at an angle, hanging from one piece of sellotape. The flat is right at the top of the block. Nell trudges up the cold staircase in her heavy boots and inhales the smells of communal life: cooking, urine, bleach. She's breathing heavily by the time she gets to the fourteenth floor. Her mother's flat is at the end of a long, bleak corridor. She hopes Sarah had visitors, despite her gut telling her otherwise.

The key turns easily in the lock and she opens the door slowly, not sure she wants to see inside. She has so many questions. Did Sarah die in her flat, and if so where? She shudders at the thought. Having spent years with no information, she now wants to hoover up every crumb, no matter how painful. She touches the necklace, which she hasn't taken off since she received it, and enters the flat.

Minimalist is the word she would use to describe it, but she doesn't think Sarah was following a trend with her interior decor aspirations. Her lack of possessions was inspired by necessity. Several rooms lead off a narrow corridor and a large living room with huge windows opens onto a balcony. A small television sits on a sideboard, the beige carpet is worn but clean and there is a battered leather sofa. She crosses to the window and looks out over the impressive view of London. Clusters of buildings small and tall crammed into every possible space. The door to the balcony is locked and a key lies on the windowsill.

The galley kitchen is dark and she switches the light on. A quick inspection of the fridge reveals an old block of cheese and some unopened milk, past the sell-by date. A cupboard contains the basics, and every surface is bare and clean. Nell feels a surge of pride that her mother looked after her flat; if only she could have taken care of herself as well.

Her anger rises as she goes into the bedroom, where a single bed dressed in a faded duvet is the centrepiece of the room. A black Venetian blind is pulled down, but it's still dark once she's opened it, so she switches the light on instead, a paper lampshade hanging from the centre of the room. A white wooden wardrobe contains her mother's clothes, and Nell takes out a winter coat and holds the material close to her face, hoping the smell will bring her mother closer, but although she inhales a faint trace of tobacco and wool, there is nothing distinctive, nothing to awaken the sensory memory she hoped for. It kills her not to have any memory of this woman who gave birth to her, as if she helped contribute to the general neglect she lived in.

Back in the living room, she opens a window and drinks from her water bottle to ease the dryness of her throat. She takes out the basic cleaning materials she has brought with her and starts on the kitchen. She disposes of the contents of jars and bottles, pours away the stinky milk and collects the containers in a bag for recycling. Then she scrubs the worktops and cupboards and the inside of the fridge. The smell of rotting rubbish is superseded by the smell of bleach. She listens to music on the radio via her phone while she works, attempting to keep at bay the sadness that keeps rising to her throat. She takes the same approach to difficult tasks she has to tackle at work: get the job done as efficiently and quickly as possible and deal with emotions and moods later.

Kitchen finished, she makes herself a black coffee from a jar she's found in a cupboard and tackles the sideboard under the television. The two shelves are full of letters and files: the details of Sarah's life. It is here that she hopes to gather some clues to her mother's personality. She knows it is most likely to be a collection of bills and information, but she holds on to the belief that there will be something here that will lead her to her mother, help her know who she was, the essence of her.

A loud noise startles her – raised male voices outside in the corridor, kids most likely. The greyness of the flat merges into the grey skies and buildings outside and she jumps to her feet, wanting to get away from here. She tucks her mother's papers into the satchel she has brought with her. Once she has made sure she hasn't overlooked anything, she locks the door and triple-checks it's secure before leaving the rubbish bags against the wall, the smell of decaying food making her gag. Sarah's flat is in the corner and there is only one flat next door to hers. The name Peters is on the letter box. She rings the doorbell and steps back, heart knocking.

This could be a waste of time, or she could be about to learn more about her mother.

An elderly man opens the door. He's wearing a short-sleeved shirt and flannel trousers. He looks wary. His eyes flicker to a sign outside the flat: *No canvassers, no hawkers.*

'Can I help you?' He stays partially behind the door as he speaks.

'Hello,' Nell says. 'I've come from next door, Sarah Wetherby's flat. I wondered if you knew her.'

'A little,' he says, opening the door a fraction. 'Who are you exactly?'

'Her daughter.'

The man frowns. 'I wasn't aware she had a daughter. She rarely had visitors.'

Nell sees from his expression that he disapproves of a daughter who never visited her mother.

'I've only just found out about her. I was adopted,' she says. It's an easier explanation than the truth.

'Ah,' he says, his shoulders relaxing, and he opens the door wider. 'You can't be too careful. I thought you were canvassing for the election. Although your resemblance to Sarah is uncanny. Would you like to come in?'

His words make her catch her breath. 'Thanks,' she says, and follows him into a warm room as crowded as her mother's was sparse. China ornaments cover every surface and fill a cabinet. She sits on a large armchair, perching on the edge so she doesn't sink into the soft cushions. A smell of shepherd's pie comes from the kitchen.

'My wife, Moira, could tell you more about poor Sarah, but she's out at the moment. I'm Tom, by the way.'

'Had you known Sarah long?'

'Oh, years. She was here when we first moved in. We didn't know her well, you understand; she kept herself to herself. Moira was more of a concerned neighbour than a friend as such.'

'You're the first person I've met who knew her at all. Until last week I didn't even know where she was. I'm trying to piece together what happened to her, find out what she was like. Do you know much about her? Anything would help.'

'She worked as a cleaner, lots of irregular shifts. Early mornings mostly, but sometimes she worked evenings too. Like I said, she hardly ever had any visitors. This past year Moira was worried about her, said she thought she was ill. She'd lost weight – and she didn't have much to lose. She was like a little bird, not very tall, with wispy blonde hair. I can see you're her daughter all right; you have the same build, and those unusual grey eyes.'

His mention of the likeness once again moves her and she swallows back tears. 'She left me this,' Sarah says, opening the locket. 'It's the only photo I've ever seen of her. But she was young here.'

Tom nods. 'She looked a lot older than that last time I saw her, unfortunately. But she had a hard life. She didn't earn much, never went away as far as I know. Never any trouble either. Moira thinks she had depression, because sometimes we didn't see her for ages and when we did she had a blank look in her eyes. We also wondered if she'd lost her job recently, as I'm always up at six and used to hear her getting up, like clockwork she was. Thin walls here, you understand. I wish I could tell you a happier story, but…'

'It's fine, the solicitor warned me. Was she friendly with anyone else in the block?'

'Not that I'm aware of. You'd be better off speaking to my wife. Will you be coming back?'

'Possibly. I've cleared the flat, but the landlord will probably want to check it over.' She gets up. 'Thanks so much. Could you tell me where to put the rubbish?'

'There's a cupboard on the ground floor; go left at the bottom of the stairs. Lift's still out, but you'll have realised that. You'll need a key, though.'

'I've got these.' She shows him the keys the solicitor gave her. He picks one out.

'That's the one. Take our number,' he adds. 'In case you don't come back.' He goes inside. Nell picks up the rubbish, and the fetid smell wafts into her face. Tom comes back with a number written on a piece of paper.

'Thank you. I'd like to speak to your wife. I'll be in touch,' she says. She wants to be away from this dark, oppressive corridor, which is drying out her throat, and Tom's unexpected kindness is making it somehow worse.

'I know Moira will be sorry to miss you. We never had kids of our own and she liked to mother Sarah – if only she'd have let her.'

The stench is multiplied in the rubbish cupboard, and flies spring out of the bin as Nell throws the bags inside. She can't get out of there fast enough. She stops off at a small public square, relieved to be out in the fresh air, away from the onslaught of smells. She sits on a bench and phones the landlord.

'I've cleared the flat,' she says. 'I wanted to know about the rent. Is there an outstanding balance, how does it work?'

'Oh, you don't need to worry about that,' he says.

'But I assumed there would be some bills to settle.'

'Bills, yes, but I've taken care of those. The rent and council tax is all paid up, though. She never had to worry about that, because she didn't pay it herself.'

'Oh, you mean she was on housing benefit?'

'No. She had a… a benefactor, I suppose you'd call it. Her rent has been paid ever since she first moved in. Hang on a minute, I can give you the details. I probably should have told the solicitor, but it slipped my mind. Sarah's death was a shock, and I've had that much on lately.'

The line goes quiet and Nell hears him rustling some papers.

'Here we are. Lilian Wetherby, that's her name. She's the one who's been paying the rent. Would you like me to give you her details?'

CHAPTER FOUR

1989

Sarah Henderson twists her engagement ring, angling it so that it catches the light from the candle burning on the table in front of her. The white cotton tablecloth has a pattern of embroidered flowers around the edge, each connected to the next by the stem, the way she and David are now connected. A swoop of joy flickers inside her like the candlelight. How can this be? She, Sarah Henderson, is engaged to be married to David Wetherby.

David. Just thinking about him makes her feel dreamy. She conjures up his face for the hundredth time today and pictures his brown eyes, framed by thick brows, his dark brown hair cropped short and gelled into spikes – he's good looking enough to get away with this cheeky hairstyle – and his dimples, which he hates and she loves. His eyes have that vulnerable look short-sighted people get, but he's resisting her attempts to persuade him to get his eyesight checked. He thinks glasses will make him look nerdy; she thinks he'll look good whatever he wears. Distinguished, she tells him; intellectual, not nerdy.

'Sarah.' A rustle of clothes and a hint of sandalwood and the imagined face dissolves into the real thing. She's on her feet and in his arms, resting her head on his chest for a fleeting second before he kisses her, then they're seated at the table, holding hands, and the waitress who is about to approach with a menu smiles and goes to another table instead.

'You're not late,' Sarah says, a smile playing on her mouth.

'I came straight from work.'

'Oh?' David's mother normally insists he pops home to check in with her, never mind that he's twenty years old and she's rich enough to have several maids to look after her, should she wish to. Sarah feels her shoulders tense and shakes them loose; she is determined that this evening Lilian's presence won't be hovering over them like a ghost as it usually is. She tells herself it's sweet that David cares so much about his mother, that it's because he's a good man, but she can't help the niggle of resentment that is deeply lodged inside her. She pushes it back down as the waitress comes over and they place their orders.

Tonight they're going for the whole experience – three courses plus aperitifs *and* coffees – because tonight is special. They've set aside this time to discuss what happens after the wedding, which is taking place next month. They're going to talk about their future life, and Sarah finds herself spiralling with excitement at the mere thought of it.

They save the main conversation and the big decisions for later, and over starters they talk about their days.

'How was your day?' she asks him, wanting to hear every detail of his time spent training in the law, hoping one day to become a barrister. She still pinches herself that such an intelligent, kind man wants to marry her.

'Five lectures back to back,' he says, and runs his hands through his hair in the way he does when he's tired, dark shadows under his eyes from late nights studying. David doesn't just want to be a solicitor; he wants to be a top barrister, the one everybody wants to fight their case. 'I had to drink a strong coffee this afternoon to stop myself falling asleep mid lecture. Can you imagine if I can't get a job at the end of this?'

'You will,' she says as she's done a hundred times before. 'We just have to be patient.' They eat in companionable silence for a few minutes. She tells him about the eventful day she's had in the doctor's surgery where she works on reception. 'I had to ring for two emergency ambulances this morning before ten thirty, which meant every appointment was running at least an hour late after that. I missed my lunch break again.'

'Make sure you claim it back,' David says, and she smiles and twists her engagement ring, fondling the diamond, never tiring of the way it sparkles when it catches the light.

'I don't mind,' she says. Nothing bothers her too much at the moment – she's in love, and it's a heady feeling; that floating-on-a-cloud feeling that she was sceptical about until it happened to her.

Once the main course has been cleared away, David asks the waitress to delay dessert. He refreshes their wine glasses and leans forward.

'So,' he says, 'I've been thinking.'

'So have I,' she says.

She's been dying to share her ideas with him, but they agreed they'd wait until this evening, the eighteen-month anniversary of the day he first took her out. She's kept the cinema ticket from that first night at the local Odeon, though she can't remember anything about the film itself. A romantic comedy, she vaguely recalls, but she was too conscious of the romance unfurling in her own life: the gorgeous man next to her who she'd had her eye on for weeks. She knew even then it was the beginning of something special.

'I've worked out on my salary we'll have to live in a flat at first. There are some one-bedroom flats on the new estate that are really nice and quite spacious. I've got some savings.' The savings are a secret she's kept from him, an inheritance from her parents. She wants to make her offer first without assuming his mother will lend or even give them a deposit, though Lilian can certainly afford it. She doesn't want David to think she's relying on him – after all, he is a student and will be for the next few years. 'Enough for a small deposit.'

She sits back, triumphant, but David has his serious face on, and her vision of their future wobbles. This wasn't the way she imagined he would react when she went through the scenario in her mind.

'Owning our own place is what we're aiming for,' he says, 'but we don't want to rush into anything. It's all very well buying a flat we can afford now, but wouldn't it be better to wait until we've saved up more money so we can get a bigger place? We both want children…' Sarah's stomach flutters at the mention of children, that excitement again: for them, for their future family, for how they're both on the same wavelength. She can already imagine the children: one boy and one girl playing in the back garden of their own home. 'We'd only have to move again in a few years' time.'

'But renting is wasting money; you know how I feel about that. And my studio flat is way too small.' Knocking against one another in the tiny room with the foldaway bed would take its toll on any couple, no matter how loved up they were.

David leans forward on his elbows, his eyes lively. 'Mum's made us a brilliant offer.'

Sarah has just lifted her wine glass; now she pauses, the glass held in mid-air as if she's about to make a toast, feeling a surge of elation. Lilian is going to give them a deposit! It was by no means certain; David's mother isn't the warmest person. Sarah can't work her out; sometimes she wonders whether Lilian even likes her, she's so frosty at times. She bites down on her lip but can't stop the smile that breaks out.

'David, that's brilliant.'

'Really? But I haven't told you what she's suggested.'

'Oh. I assumed you meant she's offered to pay a deposit on a better place. Like you said, it's better if we can get somewhere bigger earlier.'

'No. That's not what I meant. She's offered to let us live rent-free with her for a couple of years; long enough for us to save up. I know it's not ideal, but the house is huge and—'

'No.' Sarah realises she's still holding her glass in the air, any idea of a toast forgotten, and she drinks from it quickly, her cheeks as red as the wine she gulps down. 'I'm grateful, of course,' she says, but she isn't. Her insides are churning at the inevitability of what Lilian has proposed, this mother who never wants to let her son from her sight. Her stomach is clenched now and she grits her teeth, anxious not to show that she's on the verge of tears, her feelings welling up inside her. She must be careful what she says to him; she doesn't want to be rude about his mother, but she has to be firm. Lilian has a way of not accepting no for an answer, especially where David is concerned.

The waitress appears with the dessert menu, but the space Sarah had left in her stomach for the chocolate mousse she was looking forward to is now full of pebbles. She shakes her head, and, sensing a change in the mood, David asks for the bill.

'Let's walk back,' he says, taking her hand once they've been helped into their coats and are standing outside in the cold wind. 'I know you had your heart set on our own place, but two years will fly by, honestly. Tell me what you're thinking.'

They take their time strolling back to his house – Lilian's house; Sarah can never imagine calling it home, it's far too grand. Detached and set back from the road, six bedrooms and three bathrooms, with large reception rooms and entrance hall. She has got lost on more than one occasion. She tries to put into words the way Lilian makes her feel, the lack of emotion and the coldness she displays the moment David leaves the room.

'It's as if she wants you all to herself,' she says, hating that she sounds like a child but also knowing that what she says is true.

'I'm all she's got,' he says. 'It's only since Dad died that she's been like this.'

'I miss your dad,' Sarah says, a wave of sadness overtaking her. Gerald's sudden death from a heart attack had hit her hard, considering she hadn't known him that long. He'd been an ally, soft where Lilian was sharp. Living in David's family home would have been less daunting with him around.

'It will be different once we're married, I promise you.'

She hesitates and he takes her hands. 'I'll talk to Mum. See if I can persuade her to change her mind. Making you happy is the most important thing for me. Come on, you're shivering. Let's hurry back and get a coffee; we can chat some more then. Mum will have gone to bed by now.'

But yellow light spills from the house when they get back, and Lilian opens the door to them, pulling David into her arms, her cold blue eyes looking away from her son's fiancée.

'Sarah,' she says, inclining her head in acknowledgement before placing a possessive hand on David's back and following him into the lounge. A gust of cold wind blows into Sarah's face, making her eyes smart as she closes the front door behind her.

CHAPTER FIVE

2019

Nell wakes early after a fitful sleep, anxiety and rage alternate bedfellows. She spent most of the night going over and over what had happened in such a short space of time. How could one letter be such a catalyst for change, catapulting her life into turmoil?

She was tempted to ring her grandmother last night, flushed with wine and the fire of anger ignited in her belly. But she stopped herself; this quest is too important to her, she has to get it right. An alcohol-fuelled confrontation would only give Lilian ammunition against her. First she needs to check through her mother's paperwork, to confirm what the landlord told her. She knows he's right, but what she doesn't understand is why.

Outside, a light rain is falling, but the flat feels oppressive, too quiet, and she picks up the satchel containing the papers and heads off to her favourite café.

She chooses a large table at the back with room for her laptop and the papers she wants to spread out in front of her. She hopes the café will quieten down once the commuter rush is over, but for now she joins the queue of people clutching their reusable cups of different shapes and sizes. She hands her own cup over and orders a strong coffee and a Danish pastry to sustain her through the task ahead. Her head feels clear despite the lack of sleep, and chatting to the friendly staff takes her out of herself into the warmth of the café. With her mood lifted, she is confident she can shake off her tiredness.

While she eats her pastry, she logs on to her laptop and does a search for Sarah Wetherby. It jars her to think that this precious name belonged to an individual who breathed in the same London air as Nell herself, and the thought is so huge it engulfs her and makes her want to weep. The whole time she was living in Willow House with Lilian, her mother was stuck in that flat.

Just thinking about the house reminds her how she used to linger at the end of the school day, the last to leave the library before reluctantly taking the bus home. The iciness of the cavernous hallway when she stepped inside, her footsteps too loud in the silence of the house. Comparing her home with her friends who lived with noisy families, forever complaining about their brothers and sisters, made her feel guilty. Her grandmother meant well, she could see that, but her overprotectiveness drove Nell insane.

For now, she pulls her attention back to her mother. The search brings up many hits, but the tug in the pit of her stomach tells her that her mother wasn't the type to have a social-media presence – there was no laptop or PC in her flat, and the mobile Nell found there was a basic model from the days when a phone was something to make calls on and nothing else. She had hoped it might contain some kind of clue, but it doesn't appear to be working. The thought upsets her, and she abandons the Internet search and concentrates on her pastry, which is delicious and sweet, boosting her energy.

A group of chatty women have just departed and the café settles into the rhythm of the morning. Laptops are opened and freelancers begin work. Normally Nell likes to guess the profession of her fellow café-goers – the woman with the thick-rimmed glasses tapping feverishly in the opposite corner has the air of a writer. But this morning she turns her attention to the papers and begins to sort them out.

After half an hour she has built up a pile of bills, mostly red. These she will need to speak to the landlord about, check they really are all sorted. She arranges to visit the flat in a couple of weeks' time. Amongst the letters is one telling Sarah she has failed to attend a hospital appointment. Nell wonders why. It's from an oncology department, and that feels ominous. She googles oncology to make sure, and her fears are confirmed. She scans Sarah's bank statements; the landlord was right when he said she didn't pay the rent. But why was Lilian paying it? And why did Sarah walk away from her home – and her child? Nell cannot get over this hurdle. Losing her husband must have made her mother deranged with grief. When she herself split with Sam, the sadness she felt took her by surprise. And they'd only been together a year. She can't imagine how Sarah's loss must have felt in comparison.

The day Nell left home is as clear to her as if it was yesterday, the memory forever imprinted in her mind. She'd just turned sixteen, had waited until her sixteenth birthday before making the move, knowing she had more rights at that age but unable to hold on until she was eighteen, adulthood with all its promises beckoning was just too far away.

Her plans had taken shape over the last year. The job at the florist's in Seahurst had helped her save enough to live on in London for a short while. Her best friend at school, Molly, had made everything easier. Her older sister had left her London flat vacant for three months and hadn't had time to secure a lodger. Molly had given Nell the keys, and now she'd have a base rather than chancing her luck when she got there, which was her original intention. Anything would be better than spending another moment in that woman's company.

On the day itself, a Friday night, she came straight home from school and spent an hour doing her homework, playing the part. After dinner, she feigned a headache and told her grandmother she'd be going to bed early. That was no different to any other evening; she spent most evenings alone in her room while her grandmother listened to the radio downstairs. But Friday night was Lilian's Women's Institute night and she would be out until ten.

She didn't take much with her; she didn't want to alert her grandmother and had been smuggling her few possessions over to Molly's every Saturday when she went to work. She would miss Molly. She'd miss Alison, who ran the florist's, too, along with the chat with the customers and the creativity; she'd discovered a talent for creating beautiful flower displays, and dressing the shop window was her favourite part of her day. She'd contact Alison eventually, but only once it was safe to do so and she was sure she wouldn't be given away. She knew Molly would keep her secret; she wouldn't want to reveal her own part in the plot, or get her sister into trouble.

To the inhabitants of Seahurst, Lilian Wetherby was an asset: a pillar of the community, tragically widowed. She was a long-standing member of the Women's Institute and had organised more cake sales and charity events than she could remember. Feared for her forthright manner yet admired for her ability to stand up for what she believed in, Lilian got things done, and that was generally seen as a good thing for the village. She'd been instrumental in stopping the expansion of the motorway, which would have had a serious impact on certain residents. When Gerald Wetherby passed on from a massive heart attack, she held her head high, wore black for a week and organised the funeral and memorial with breathtaking efficiency. Afterwards, she rarely mentioned him in public. Lilian was not one to let the small matter of her husband's death curtail her activities.

She was held in such high esteem that nobody would dare openly question her parenting skills, but there was some agreement amongst the women, behind closed doors and in confidence, that they felt a tad sorry for the granddaughter Lilian had brought up as her own after 'that business'. For anyone could see Lilian was too protective. Naturally she provided very well for her charge – Nell attended the best school, had beautiful manners and was always impeccably dressed – but the girl didn't look happy. As Annie Williams remarked to Alison Shaftesbury, 'She doesn't let the poor child out of her sight. But it's understandable, given what happened.' It was Annie who suggested to Alison when she was looking for a Saturday assistant that a chance like this might bring young Nell out of herself, though even Annie was surprised at how creative the girl turned out to be, designing the most beautiful window displays.

It was only later, after Nell had so suddenly left home, that Lilian showed a crack in her icy exterior, admitting to Annie that she hadn't given her granddaughter enough space to grow. And it was many months after that that Alison told Annie how the girl had begun confiding in her, and that it hadn't surprised her at all that Nell had upped and left. 'The child had ambition,' she said, 'and she's a tough cookie, very independent.' Which gave Annie Williams much to think about.

Nell will never forget the kindness of Molly and her sister, but the guilt she feels at leaving her grandmother so suddenly is always there too. That last row they had, when Lilian made plain her objection to Nell's ambition to set up her own business, and refused to help her move away from Seahurst and train, Nell could see her future disappearing before her eyes. She knew it was time to act. Leaving of her own accord seemed like the only possibility.

She got back in touch with Lilian once she'd given her time to get over the shock, waited until she'd found herself somewhere to live and got a job in an office, putting on hold her dream to train as a florist – paying the rent was the most important thing. Lilian guilt-tripped her every time she called, saying how much she missed her and reminding her of what she'd sacrificed to bring her up.

Nell tried to talk about her job, her friends, the life she was building for herself, even invited her to come and visit, but Lilian insisted she wasn't well enough to travel, was too miserable, tried to press whichever of Nell's buttons she was focusing on that week. After every conversation Nell felt the need to go out and mainline gin with Hannah and the gang.

Back home that afternoon, she cleans the flat from top to bottom before she dials the number she still knows off by heart.

'It's Nell here,' she says, without giving her grandmother the chance to speak first.

But it's a male voice that answers.

'Hello, could I speak to Lilian Wetherby,' Nell says, keeping her voice calm.

'Lil's not living here any more.'

Lil. Her grandmother would be horrified at this abbreviation. A sense of unease prickles at her scalp. Lilian can't have sold up, not without telling her, surely? She would never loosen her grip on Willow House; it's been in the family for years.

'What? Who are you?'

The line goes dead.

Nell is still gripping the phone, knuckles white, a sense of dread rendering her unable to move.

CHAPTER SIX

2019

Nell steps onto the train to a loud beeping noise as the door closes behind her. She walks through two carriages before locating a seat, though she has to squeeze past a large man sitting in the aisle seat, leaving her little room, her rucksack clutched on her lap. Packing was easy; most of her clothes are black or grey, so she can mourn her mother with dignity.

She closes her eyes and allows her heartbeat to slow down. She tried the house several times after the first attempt, but the phone rang and rang and nobody picked up. The subsequent phone conversation with the solicitor made her late, and she ended up having to run to the station. The rhythm of the train normally calms her, but this time she's too wired to relax.

Familiar sights flash past as the train speeds up on her journey to discover the past she's only just uncovered. She hears the rattle of the refreshment trolley and buys herself a coffee to keep her mind alert. Ringing the solicitor merely heightened her fears; he'd heard nothing from her grandmother and had no idea who it might have been that answered the phone.

All sorts of possibilities are occurring to her. Squatters have moved into the house. The mystery man is a con artist who has hoodwinked her grandmother into handing over her life savings. The locket rests against her chest, safe underneath a black roll-neck jumper.

*

It's been years since Nell last visited Seahurst. She walks down to the seafront, enjoying the fresh air, the fragrance of seaweed and salt, so different from the city fumes, which clog her chest and make her feel as if she is permanently suffering from hay fever. A seagull swoops down in front of her and perches on a piece of driftwood on the stony beach, watching her as if assessing what she's doing here. Nell used to come here every Saturday after her day at the florist's and throw pebbles in the sea she loved to swim in, wishing she had known her parents. The maternal florist was kind to her and she didn't know how to deal with it.

She will never forget the second time she confronted her grandmother and demanded to know about her mother and father. She was thirteen. A letter from school had triggered it, a letter beginning 'Dear Parents'. Nowadays, her teacher friend Jo has confirmed, such insensitivity wouldn't be allowed; non-discriminatory terms such as 'carer' would be used instead. Nell welcomes this, but whether it would have averted the ensuing scene is doubtful; the need to know about her heritage had been bubbling inside her for years.

She watched her classmates folding their letters, shoving them into oversized bags; their worries were focused on what the teachers were going to say at the upcoming parents' evening, how much trouble they'd be in. Nell wondered what teachers thought when her grandmother appeared, tall and imposing, with her severe wardrobe and imperious attitude. Lilian's standards were exacting and she'd grill the teachers on what exactly they were doing to get the most out of her granddaughter. Nell would cringe beside her, watching others with kind-looking mothers and interested fathers, parents who cared, an affectionate arm slung around a child's shoulder, a shared smile.

When she was younger, Nell used to ask questions about her extended family, but this was one of the many issues Lilian clammed up about. 'The past doesn't interest me,' she would say. 'The present is what matters.' Meanwhile Nell would devour historical novels from the town library and lose herself in another time, where she slayed dragons and embarked on magical quests and had the freedom to go wherever she wanted, answering to no one. At school she was team captain, form monitor; she revelled in being part of a group.

That evening, she went straight home from school, giving netball club a miss. When Lilian asked to see what homework she'd been given, she unfolded the letter and told her she wanted to ask her some questions. Lilian sat down opposite her. Nell was shaking with passion, so great was her desire to know. She'd dug deep into her innermost feelings, the feelings she glossed over at school, shrugging off her friends' curious questions: did she mind about not having parents? About being brought up by an old person? She laughed it all off and saw the admiration in their eyes at how strong she was. 'It hurts me like a long needle digging into my skin every time I think about not knowing,' she told Lilian now, quoting the words she'd scribbled in her diary when the needle was at its sharpest and causing her maximum pain. 'So I want to know exactly what happened. I can take it.'

Lilian regarded her solemnly, small blue eyes over her hawkish nose, and told her about the car accident in which her parents had died. Her father David had been driving; Lilian had witnessed the whole thing, watching in horror as the brakes failed and he lost control of the car. Both David and Sarah, Nell's mother – 'Such a sweet woman,' she said with unaccustomed tenderness, her voice quavering slightly – had died immediately when the car had crashed into a large tree, David crushed against the steering wheel and Sarah against the windscreen; there had been no airbags in the car. She clasped her hands together, her interlaced fingers trembling. Nell took those hands, untwisting them in a rare moment of physical contact, and Lilian didn't stop her.

'Tell me more about my mother,' she asked, but tears brimmed in Lilian's eyes and she shook her head, her mouth quivering.

'I can't,' she whispered, and Nell understood it was too painful for her. Now, though, now that she knows the truth about her mother, she wonders whether her grandmother was spinning a sticky web around her, capturing her with lies. If so, it's time to unravel them.

Anxiety returns as she waits at the bus stop, the route to real life as she used to see it when she lived here. This bus took her to school and her friends, then back to the house she saw as a prison. Again she thinks of Sarah, taking the same route, but were her feelings the same? Life in London didn't turn out well for her; unlike Nell, who cherishes the small but tight circle of friends who have replaced her family. She hopes she can uncover some happiness in her mother's story.

It's a ten-minute walk to the house along a country lane, past the tiny grocer's shop – which she is amazed to see is still there – up the hill and a sharp turn left onto a narrow path. The large gate is hidden by trees, the house set back from its neighbours and twice the size. The doorbell is loud and she steps back to survey the front of the house. Paint is peeling from the doors and windows and the greenery in the front garden is mostly weeds. Would Lilian have let it get into such a state? She hops from foot to foot, straining to hear a sound. The sound she does hear is unexpected, car tyres on gravel, and she turns to see a small white van coming up the drive. A man jumps out. He's in his thirties, tanned, wearing jeans, a checked flannel shirt and muddy boots.

'Can I help you?' he asks. His accent sounds local and she thinks it's the voice from the phone. He looks wary as he takes her in, eyes lingering on her backpack, which she's deposited on the floor.

'We spoke on the phone.' He stares at her, frowning. 'You hung up on me. I've come to see Lilian.'

He locks the van with a jab at his fob and the gravel crunches as he approaches.

'I've already told you she's not here.'

'And I've told you I need to speak to her.' Heat spreads up her neck and she's grateful that the roll-neck jumper hides the blush that always develops when she's nervous. 'It's urgent, family business.'

'So tell me. I'm family.'

'No offence, but I have no idea who you are.'

'Same here.'

They stare at one another until Nell flings her hands up in exasperation.

'I'm Nell, Lilian's granddaughter.'

'The long-lost granddaughter. Of course.'

'Who are you?'

'Adam Harris. I'm her great-nephew.'

'Great-nephew? But…' Nell racks her brains. Then she recalls Lilian's sister Glenys, a dim memory from when she was about six, a blazing row and a slamming door.

'Are you related to Glenys?'

'I am indeed. My mum Denise is her daughter. Not being funny, but how do I know you are who you say you are? It's not as if Lilian has any photos of you, like most doting grandmothers.'

'She hates photos. I don't know why. My father was Lilian's son David and he was killed in a car crash. I left home at sixteen. I used to live here; I went to St Winifred's School, as did Lilian. You can contact her solicitor, Mr Grayling, if you don't believe me. Your mum would know I'm telling the truth. Look, can we go inside? I'd love a cup of tea. I've just travelled up from London and I could do with using the bathroom.'

'Tea?' He stares at her as if she's suggested they drink bleach together. 'I'm in the middle of something. I'm doing some work on the house.'

She hoists her rucksack onto her shoulders. 'I can wait. It's not a problem. Please.'

'I suppose it can't do any harm,' he says, and opens the door. Behind him Nell sees the dark entrance hall like the mouth of a cave, and a cold feeling makes her shiver.

Adam goes inside, his boots leaving a trail of mud on the patterned tiles. Nell follows him in, then comes to a halt, the strangest feeling taking hold of her, like stepping back in time. The painting, her painting, still hangs on the wall, and she rests her hand on the banister to steady herself. Alison from the florist's gave it to her for her sixteenth birthday. Alison, her surrogate mother, so warm compared to the grandmother who loved her but could only show it by smothering her.

She catches a glimpse of the drawing room, as gloomy as she remembers it, heavy velvet curtains framing the windows, but Adam goes through to the kitchen and she breathes out, relieved. He dumps a carrier bag on the counter and takes out a loaf of sliced white bread and a box of eggs. He's living here then. Alone, she imagines, as the kitchen is free of any signs of the presence of a woman.

'Tea?' he asks. 'Or coffee?' He takes a jar of instant coffee from the cupboard and presents it like a challenge.

Nell has been spoilt in London, with artisan coffee shops on every corner. She can't help thinking of the instant coffee she drank in Sarah's flat and pushes the thought away.

'Tea, please.' She sits at the table without waiting to be asked. She's suddenly exhausted from the journey and hunger gripes at her stomach. She sizes Adam up as he puts tea bags into mugs and opens the milk. He has the rough hands of a builder, face tanned from working outside. He takes a packet of custard creams from the cupboard and shoves one in his mouth, leaving the packet open on the table. Lilian always had custard creams in the house, and Nell's throat seizes up at the memory.

He takes another biscuit and eats it in two bites. He puts a mug of tea in front of her.

'If you're her granddaughter, why haven't you been around more? She's not been well for ages and could have done with some help. Me and my partner have done everything for her. It's not easy, you know, and we've got two kids to look after.'

'I'm sorry to hear that,' Nell says. 'It's been difficult with me and Gran.' The word sounds wrong, but to call her Lilian as she always has might confuse him. 'Her solicitor wasn't able to get hold of her, which is why I'm here. Perhaps you spoke to him?'

'I don't remember. I'm very protective of Aunt Lil.'

'So where is she exactly? If you give me her address, I'll go and see her.'

'What is it you want?' He brushes biscuit crumbs from his T-shirt.

'I've got some news for her from the solicitor.' It's not strictly true, but she's determined to get past him.

'I can pass it on.'

'I want to see her.' *To make sure she's safe.* 'I'm her granddaughter.'

'Bit late to be playing that card, isn't it?'

Nell breathes in deeply, trying not to let him rile her.

'Yes, it is, I know. But I'm here now and I'm not going back until I've seen her. I was hoping I could stay for a few days, while I sort things out with her.'

'What, here?' He pulls a face.

'Yes. I grew up here, you know. This used to be my home.'

'Doesn't make any difference. I'll have to speak to Lil.'

'Can't you give me her address so I can ask her myself?'

'No need, I'll give her a call. Wait here.' He pulls his mobile from his pocket and takes it out into the back garden.

Nell looks down at the wooden kitchen table where she used to do her homework. She runs her hand down the table leg until she feels the change in the wood, her initials carved into it. Adam comes back, hitching his jeans up.

'I can't get hold of her,' he says. 'I'll keep trying.'

'I can prove who I am,' Nell says, pushing her chair back, pointing to the table leg. 'Look under here. I left my mark when I was thirteen, when Gran was out. My teenage rebellion.'

'NW,' Adam reads.

'Nobody else would know that was there. Lilian never saw it – I wasn't that brave.' She grins.

'I guess so. Well, you can stay tonight, seeing as you've come all this way. It's not as if we're short of bedrooms. I'm using the one at the top of the house.'

'Is your partner here too?'

'No, just me.'

'OK.' Nell says it brightly to hide her sense of unease. Is she being reckless, staying here with this man she doesn't know? She's proved who she is, but she hasn't required the same of him. 'Thanks. I'll take my old room. It's the one next to the master bedroom.'

Adam picks up a bag of tools from the floor. 'I need to get on.'

'What exactly are you doing?'

'I'm converting the whole of the ground floor, making it accessible for Lilian. I'm turning the downstairs loo into a proper bathroom, an en suite next to the dining room which will become the bedroom. I'll knock down the kitchen wall into the front room and make an open-plan kitchen and living room. She'll use the front entrance and I'm creating an entrance through the back to the upstairs part of the house. I'll be...' He stops. 'That's it, basically.'

'It sounds good.' She wants to ask him more about Lilian's health, unable to imagine her grandmother ageing, but he's already going out into the garden. She watches him take his phone out and make a call. He paces about, glancing over at her more than once, as if checking whether she's still there.

Nell sits on her childhood bed and opens the window. She'd forgotten how it felt to live in such a large house, the high ceilings and wide corridors so different to her London flat. It would have been a perfect place for a game of hide-and-seek, had she ever had anyone to play with. The sound of drilling fills the room from downstairs, where Adam is working.

She unpacks her few belongings and sets them out, then heads back down to the kitchen and checks the contents of the fridge. She decides to go and get some shopping in town. She wants to let Adam know she's going out as a matter of courtesy, and that she needs a key, though she doubts he'll agree to that. She goes outside.

Adam sees her but takes his time smoothing the edge of a piece of wood he's been sawing on a workbench. Finally he takes off the protective eyewear he's wearing.

'Did you want something?' He wipes sweat from his forehead.

'I need to speak to Lilian, urgently.' She wants him to know she won't give up.

'You already said. I'll keep trying to get hold of her.'

'I want to go and see her. Why won't you tell me where she is?'

'See it from my point of view. You turn up after who knows how long and expect to drop right back into her life.'

'We have been in touch, you know, just not very often.' Her face colours. 'I just want to know she's safe.'

'Safe?' He barks out a short laugh. 'Of course she's safe. OK, I'll spell it out for you. She might not want to see you; that's why I want to check with her first.' He lowers his mask back over his eyes.

'I'm going into the village to get some food. I don't have a key. Is there one I can borrow?'

'I suppose you can take the spare. It's hanging by the front door.'

'OK. Well I'll see you later, I guess.'

He doesn't respond, and the sound of sawing resumes as she walks back into the house.

CHAPTER SEVEN

2019

Nell heads for the village square, which is little changed by the intervening years. One pub, a post office, a bakery and a small supermarket. The dairy is gone, though, and there's a café in its place. She wonders whether the florist's is still there, and crosses the street to take a look. Shutters are pulled down over the windows and the sign that used to read *Alison's Petals* is now obscured by a board marked *FOR SALE. Fairfield and Evans.* Another name from her past. She heads over to the post office. A bell rings as she enters and a middle-aged woman behind the counter calls out a cheery hello.

'Hi,' Nell says, amazed at how unchanged the place is. The same small counter behind a glass partition at the end of the shop, the only difference being that they now sell pay-as-you-go phone cards.

'I haven't seen you around here before,' the woman says. Nell doubts she would recognise the young girl who yearned for more excitement than a post office and a village pub could offer.

'It's been a while,' she says. 'I'm visiting Mrs Wetherby, who used to live at Willow House. Do you know her?'

A strange expression crosses the woman's face, quickly erased. 'Oh indeed,' she says, 'poor old Mrs Wetherby' – not a phrase Nell is accustomed to hearing – 'she's moved out, so I heard. A young man's living there, a builder; he drives a white van. He came in here once, asking questions about Lilian.'

'What kind of questions?'

'He wanted to know whether she had any friends in the village. He said she seemed very isolated.'

'And what did you tell him?'

'I didn't tell him anything, of course. He seemed pleasant enough, but you can never be too careful these days.'

And Nell is staying with this same man, who she knows nothing about. She experiences a moment of panic: what if he's lying about being Lilian's great-nephew? Should she find somewhere else to stay?

'The florist's further down – do you know when it closed?'

'About a year ago. It's been on the market ever since.'

'Shame,' Nell says, wondering what happened to Alison.

She heads towards the main street and follows the signs to the library. The high street is more lively now, with people going in and out of shops and a group of young mothers chatting around a cluster of prams. A bus pulls in, the same bus she used to travel to school in, and she recalls the first time she took that journey, standing out in her bottle-green St Winifred's uniform when every other kid wore the red and white of Challoner High. Most of the local kids went to the nearest school, which was only a mile out of town, but that wasn't good enough for Lilian, who insisted on Nell going to her own alma mater.

She shakes off the memories. Things would have been so different if she'd had a group of mates here, like the young mothers who are laughing now and saying their goodbyes, gathering their kids together. She smiles at them as she passes. Coming back here can be a different experience for her this time; she doesn't have to be imprisoned in the past. Her own friends might be in London, but these days distance doesn't matter: people are connected online now, wherever they are in the world.

In the library foyer, she stops in front of the large portrait of a former mayor of the town. That hasn't changed. Even when Nell was young, the woman was no longer mayor, the small town stuck in a time warp. The picture feels familiar, as does the building, even though self-service counters have been installed and the bright and airy space is more inviting, the wooden bookcases replaced with metal ones.

Two women are sitting at a small desk, chatting. Nell makes her way over, and a woman of about her own age with a mass of red hair pulled back into a ponytail greets her with a friendly smile.

'Hi,' Nell says, 'can you help me?'

'Oh, I don't know about that,' the woman says. She pushes her glasses up her nose and they promptly slide back down again. Her colleague smiles and goes to help another customer, who has come in behind Nell. 'But I'll do my best. What can I help you with?'

'I was hoping to do some family research.'

'Well, we have a small reference section up there.' She points towards a mezzanine level at the far end of the library, where a couple of people are studying at tables. 'It's not exactly the British Library. I'm guessing you're not from around here.'

'Actually, I was born here, but I haven't been back for years.'

'Ah, so it's local history you're wanting to do.' She smiles. 'You might just be in luck, in that case. I've got a bit of a fascination with local history, bordering on the obsessive. Librarians can be like that – goes with the job. I've done a lot of research and built up the collection, and my knowledge of the area is pretty good if I say so myself.' Her grin is infectious, and Nell smiles back.

'That's wonderful. My parents were from Seahurst, and their parents before them. I don't know much about them, and wanted to start some kind of family tree.'

'Well you're in the right place. I've done some work on my own tree and it's fascinating stuff. Once you get hooked, it's hard to stop digging. And there are lots of resources online, of course. I'd recommend joining one of the larger sites to get yourself started. They can also give you guidance on where to order documents –

birth certificates, that kind of thing. I can always help you with that too. I've pretty much reached a dead end with my tree. I'm here most days, for my sins. I'm Jenny, by the way.'

'Nell.'

They share an easy smile.

'So are you staying in the village, or just here for the day?'

'A few days at least. I'm staying at my grandmother's house.'

'In the village?'

'Yes, Willow House.'

'Oh, I know it. You must mean old Mrs Wetherby.'

'That's right.' Nell had forgotten how everyone's business is common knowledge in this tiny place. Another reason she felt stifled as a self-conscious teenager.

'Oh, are you with the builder who's moved in?'

She feels her neck flush red. 'No, I'm not.'

Jenny doesn't miss her appalled tone and raises an eyebrow.

'Oh jeez.' Nell claps a hand over her mouth. 'You don't know him, do you?'

Jenny laughs. 'I don't, but my mother makes the business of this town her own. He's not my type either.'

They share another smile. Jenny is easy to be with and Nell feels herself the most relaxed she has been in days, enjoying this conversation.

Jenny throws a quick glance at the counter, which is free of customers. 'Let me show you the reference section anyway.' Her hair bounces as she bounds up the stairs. 'Where do you live now?' she asks.

'North London, Islington.'

'I've often thought about moving away, but there's only me and my mother now. She's always telling me I'm free to go and do my own thing, but I know she's putting on a brave face. She's diabetic and I like to keep an eye on her. Mothers, eh? Still, maybe one day.'

Nell ignores the pang Jenny's comment gives her.

*

Nell spends an hour looking at the information in the library. There are numerous books on the history of the area, which look interesting, and she enjoys seeing how the town used to look, but she realises she needs to do a more specific search and build up a family tree, so she spends the rest of the time setting up an account on an ancestry site. She'll have to look around and see if there is any documentation in the house, though she doubts Adam will trust her to go through anything that's been left there. She needs to speak to Lilian, and fast, to verify that he's genuinely been left in charge. Should she be more worried than she is?

On her way out, Jenny calls her over and Nell updates her on her progress.

'I need more information to get anywhere with this family tree,' she says. Jenny's friendly, open face invites confidences, but she stops herself from blurting out the whole saga.

'I'll speak to my gran,' Jenny says. 'You know what it's like around here. She's a similar age to Mrs Wetherby and they most probably knew each other as it's such a small place. She went to the local primary school and then St Winifred's.' Nell pulls a face. 'You too?' Jenny laughs. 'I refused to go there and luckily Mum agreed. The local comprehensive isn't too bad; it's not like the inner-city schools you read about.'

'You've been really helpful, and that's so kind of you, I'd love it if you could speak to your grandmother.'

'Come back to the library soon and I'll let you know what she says.' Jenny hesitates. 'I've enjoyed talking to you.'

'Me too.'

'Maybe we could grab a coffee sometime.'

'Yes, I'd like that.'

Nell passes the framed photograph of the mayor on her way out, feeling a weird sensation as she does so, as though she's suddenly been plunged back into her teenage years. The woman's clear blue eyes seem to watch her as she leaves the library. She shakes the feeling off, pleased to have met a potential friend.

She picks up some shopping in the small supermarket on her way back to the house. It's quiet on her return and she checks the garden, but there's no sign of Adam. She unpacks the shopping, and as she makes herself a cup of peppermint tea, she fiddles with her locket – she can't stop herself from checking every now and then that it's still there. Her grandmother had no photos in the house when she was growing up, so the locket is especially precious to her now. Seeing her mother for the first time has affected her in a huge way, and a wave of desolation sweeps over her whenever she thinks about Sarah being alive all this time without her knowing. She burns to know what made Lilian hide the truth from her. Her grandmother was overprotective, but she was never cruel, and Nell can't fathom why she would do this to her. She paces up and down, unable to settle. Adam has to give her Lilian's address. Failing that, she'll think of another way of tracking her down.

She runs upstairs to the bathroom, then goes into her room to get her hairbrush and comes to a standstill. Her rucksack is lying down on the floor. Her arms erupt in goose bumps. She always leaves it standing up. It's a hangover from a time when she left a bottle of olive oil in there and it leaked all over her clothes, ruining her favourite Levi's.

Unease prickles at the back of her neck. She doesn't need to picture the scene. It's a given. She opens the wardrobe, not knowing what she's looking for, but her clothes are hanging as she left them. An unfamiliar odour tickles her nostrils; she sniffs and tries to get a sense of what it is. A fragrance of some kind? Pine? Aftershave? Adam?

Adam. What would he be looking for in her room? And what if it's not him? For whatever reason, somebody has been in her room. And she doesn't know why.

CHAPTER EIGHT

1991

Sarah pokes around in the fridge, but her skimmed milk isn't there. She sighs and takes the carton of full-fat milk and pours a small amount onto her muesli. She lingers in the kitchen, wondering whether to make the small act of rebellion by eating out in the conservatory, where she can watch the birds at the feeder outside, but Lilian made such a fuss last time. She sighs and takes the bowl and a mug of peppermint tea into the dining room, where she sits at the formal table and wishes Gerald were still around to tease her about her funny teas and how he'd like to feed her up. She swallows down the wave of sadness that rises whenever she thinks about Gerald, pulls her too-loose skirt up and makes a mental note to herself to go shopping. Her clothes don't seem to fit her any more.

Her thoughts turn to the day ahead. She's on the morning shift at the surgery today, finishing at one, and then she's planning an afternoon looking around the estate agents' in town. If she presents David with some prearranged viewings, meets him at the appointments without mentioning anything to Lilian, maybe they'll actually make some progress towards moving.

The door creaks and the noise bursts the bubble of her dream as a whiff of lavender announces Lilian's arrival in the room.

'Good morning,' she says in a cold tone that matches the frost on the grass outside. Sarah tells herself her mother-in-law speaks that way to everyone, but at that moment the cleaner appears and Lilian's voice softens as she says 'Good morning, Joyce' with a smile. Joyce has worked for the family for over ten years. Maybe it takes that long for Lilian to thaw enough to trust someone. If Sarah were to be here that long, she'd kill herself, she thinks wryly, and plasters on a smile.

'Morning, Lilian.'

Lilian nods in that imperious way of hers and pours herself a cup of coffee from the filter machine on the side. Strong and bitter is how she likes it. Joyce places the local newspaper on the table in front of her and is rewarded with another brief smile. Blink and you'd miss it.

Sarah spoons muesli into her mouth and chews as quickly as she can, convinced the noise she makes is reverberating around the room. David has left for university already – she was dimly aware of the kiss he planted on her cheek as she dozed, and she hopes he'll remember they've arranged to meet for a drink later. And fingers crossed she'll have some viewings for them to attend.

Lilian scans the headlines on the paper and pushes it to one side.

'Are you working today, Sarah?'

Sarah nods, making awkward movements with her mouth as she tries to clear it of food. A nut crunches between her teeth, making what to her sounds like a loud crack. She winces.

'Yes, this morning only, but I won't be back for lunch; I'm going shopping in town.' She changes the subject, fearing that somehow Lilian will see through the shopping ruse and stop her from beginning her property search. 'I couldn't find my skimmed milk just now,' she adds, looking her mother-in-law in the eye.

Lilian raises her eyebrows, which makes her look even haughtier. 'If it was past its sell-by date, Joyce would have got rid of it.'

'It wasn't out of date.' She's had more than one conversation about this with Joyce, who swears she doesn't touch Sarah's milk, and Sarah believes her. Joyce doesn't tell lies, unlike Lilian, who tells many – small ones, harmless ones, she will say when questioned or confronted, although Sarah rarely bothers. It's not worth it.

Lilian turns her attention back to the newspaper and Sarah stares at her thick silver hair, waved and set and sprayed just so, as immovable as her opinions.

Back in the bedroom she shares with David, she takes her calendar off the wall and counts the days she's marked off since she's been in this house. Over five hundred days – eighteen months; David promised her they'd live here for two years maximum. Once all the days are marked off, they should be in their own home.

She checks her make-up in the mirror, smooths the back of her hair, which today is swept up into a smart chignon, and pulls on the jacket that matches her skirt. That too is loose, and she resolves to stop in town after she's been to the estate agents' and treat herself to a new outfit before she meets David later.

She doesn't bother to say goodbye to Lilian, who is once again engrossed in the week's news, looking for more local occurrences to complain about. Lilian keeps a keen eye on everything that goes on in the village; as one of the leading members of the local Women's Institute, she sees herself as a person of authority. Sarah feels better able to stand up to her this morning, more confident now that she's armed with a plan. She has spent far too long in this godforsaken house; she is getting out and taking David with her.

Grosvenor's is quiet this early on a Thursday evening. David orders the drinks while Sarah looks around for a table. The bar is in a basement, with the ground floor being reserved for diners. Back at the house, Lilian is cooking dinner as she does every day; it will be served at seven o'clock on the dot, so they have one hour to discuss everything. Now that Sarah is thinking of breaking free, the restrictive schedule Lilian imposes on them seems ever more ridiculous, and she wonders if she can persuade David to push the boundaries a little, suggest eating later.

Light rain is falling outside and she shakes droplets from her coat and drapes it over a chair by a table in a cosy corner. The walls of the bar are exposed brick and a real fire burns in the fireplace. She takes out the information pack she got from the estate agent earlier, her news bubbling inside. She can't wait to share it with David.

Her husband appears with a pint for himself and a gin and tonic for her, a slice of lime arranged over the side of the glass, a packet of peanuts held between his teeth. She experiences a thrill of joy as she always does in his presence.

'You'll spoil your appetite,' she says, imitating Lilian's voice, and he laughs.

'I know you won't tell,' he says, taking a large swig of beer. 'I needed that.' He opens the nuts and scoops a handful into his mouth. 'What's all that?' He gestures towards the folder with salty fingers. 'Fairfield and Evans,' he reads. 'Isn't that…?'

'An estate agent,' she says, her smile triumphant as she leans towards him. 'I've had such a great afternoon,' she goes on, speaking fast before he can interrupt her and put a stop to her plans. 'I visited three different agents', but this one was the best. The man there was so helpful. He's arranged a couple of viewings for me, look…' She pulls out the property details, which she's arranged in the order she likes them best. 'This one here is perfect. It's a cottage, two bedrooms and… Well, see for yourself.' She hands him the sheet of paper, where the outside of the chocolate-box cottage can be seen in a glorious colour photograph. He wipes salt from his fingers before taking it, his eyelashes flickering as he skim-reads the contents.

'It looks OK,' he says, 'but a viewing? Isn't that a bit presumptuous? We haven't even decided we're ready to move.'

'It's been eighteen months,' she says, keeping her tone level to hide the exasperation she feels. 'Two years at most you said we'd be at Willow House. It's time we moved on, David, just the two of us.'

He sets the paper down on the table, face down so she can no longer see the property upon which she is pinning her hopes.

'This is about my mother, isn't it?'

Sarah sighs and her shoulders slump. Discussing Lilian is inevitable, but it never ends well. David is devoted to his mother and Sarah can't understand why, but she is devoted to David and she will make this work, she has to. She clenches her fists under the table to strengthen her resolve. She won't give in.

'Yes, it is. It's very kind of her to let us live rent-free, but we've never lived alone together as a married couple and I've had enough. No matter that the house is huge and gorgeous and… No, let me finish.' He's raised his hand as if about to speak and it's important she says her piece. She's practised what she wants to say for so long, the words come out fluently. Don't criticise his mother, she tells herself. Own your feelings; that way he'll understand. He has to know how she feels. 'I'm not happy and I haven't been for ages. I'm happy with you and me, but I've had enough waiting for us to start our married life properly. I don't feel relaxed in that house. I want for us to be able to cook our own meals, eat them whenever we want, to have a space we can decorate and make our own. I want to be carried over the threshold.' The last comment is meant to be flippant, but he isn't smiling.

'Why haven't you told me this before? I thought you were happy.'

Her chest feels tight that he hasn't even noticed, but he's so busy studying, he barely notices her when he gets home in the evening, collapsing on the sofa after dinner and watching whatever programme Lilian has picked. Sarah just wants to choose what she watches for a change. Never mind the other things Lilian does to her, making her feel like an inferior human being. David doesn't know about those and she doesn't want to go into them, now or ever. She doesn't want to lose him.

'We're lucky, you know, to be in the position we're in, with a lovely home to live in while we save up. I want our own home too, but we're not ready. We've nowhere near saved enough money.'

'That's where you're wrong. I talked to Philip about it.'

'Philip? Who's he?'

'The estate agent. We don't need as much as we thought for the deposit, and it's perfectly possible for us to get a mortgage with my savings. This property here' – she turns the paper over so the photograph is visible again – 'it might only have two bedrooms and I know we always said we wanted three, but the studio in the garden is amazing, it's like a room in itself.'

'You're not pregnant, are you?'

'No.' Colour burns her cheeks. 'And I wouldn't want to be, not while we're not in our own place. I can't relax knowing your mother is along the corridor. Even though she's not right next to us it just feels… weird.'

'Surely it would be better having Mum on tap as a babysitter.'

'No.' The words sound sharp and final, but the ones that follow spill out like water, and she's saying everything she told herself not to, how Lilian hates her and undermines her and makes her feel like she isn't herself any more. 'I used to be so confident, and now…' A tear trickles from her eye.

David looks shocked. 'Don't get upset. I had no idea. Give me a second to go to the gents', then we'll talk about it.' He glances at his watch. Don't you dare mention being late for dinner, she thinks.

By the time he gets back, she has composed herself, eyes wiped free of tears and skirt smoothed down. He gives her a hug before he sits down again.

'This is my fault,' he says. 'My course has been full-on lately and it's so easy for me to accept everything Mum does for me without considering your feelings. She's controlling, I know that.'

'She doesn't want to share you, David. She makes that clear when you're not around. I'm convinced she deliberately makes me feel unwelcome. She wants to drive me away.'

David shakes his head. 'She wouldn't. You have to understand how hard it's been for her. She would never talk about this herself – Dad explained it all to me one day. He told me never to ask her about it as she was hugely sensitive about it. She'd wanted children from an early age and they tried for a long time, but eventually, after lots of tests, which she found excruciating – she's very private, my mother – they discovered she couldn't conceive. It nearly destroyed her. She'd always wanted a son, never a daughter. When they adopted me, she saw me as her salvation, but Dad made sure I didn't become a spoilt brat and he balanced her behaviour out. If he hadn't been around, I don't think she'd ever have let me out of her sight. Since he's been gone' – he sips at his drink, sadness distorting his face for a second, and Sarah puts her hand over his – 'she's got worse, I have noticed that. But leaving her on her own isn't easy. She'd rattle around in that great big house.'

'Couldn't she move to somewhere more suitable for one person? It would make life a lot easier for her. There are some great little places for sale at the moment.' Sarah would like to live as far away from Lilian as possible, but not living together at all is the first step.

'And give up the family home? Are you crazy? She wants me to have it; it's been in the family for years. She doesn't see the point in me ever moving out, since I'll inherit anyway.'

'That could be years away,' Sarah says. David's words have filled her with horror. If Lilian plans to keep them there forever, they have to get out as soon as possible. 'You have to live your own life. *I* need to live my own life.'

She finishes her drink and looks at her watch. Ten to seven. She gets up. 'If we don't go now, Lilian will be in a mood all evening,' she says, her tone clipped. 'I can't do this any more, David. It's time for us to be a proper married couple. If you don't accept what I'm telling you, she'll get what she wants. And I have to get out of there, with or without you.'

CHAPTER NINE

2019

The front door slams and Nell jumps. She goes to the top of the stairs and looks down into the hallway. An elderly woman has let herself into the house and is taking off her coat. She has her back to Nell, who notes the head of short dark-grey hair and her small, wiry stature. Definitely not Lilian; she's way too small. Nell's pounding heart is returning to its normal beat.

'Hello,' she says, and the woman whips round, her hand flying to her chest.

'Goodness, you startled me. What are you doing here?'

'I was going to ask the same of you.'

'I'm assuming you're a friend of Adam's?' the woman says. 'I'm the cleaner, Joyce.'

Joyce. Grandmother used to talk about a woman called Joyce who worked as her cleaner, but that was years ago and Nell never met her. Could it be the same person? Close up, her face is lined and her shoulders stooped, but her eyes are alert, watchful.

'Adam didn't mention anyone would be here. Is he in?'

'I don't think so.' Nell descends the stairs. 'I'm Nell, Lilian's granddaughter.' Close up, Joyce makes her feel taller than she is.

'Nell?' Joyce narrows her eyes. 'Really? I don't believe it.' She folds her arms. 'How do I know you are who you say you are?'
How many more times?

'I've been through all this with Adam; why don't you check with him? Grandma used to talk about a Joyce who cleaned for her, but it was before I was born. Was that you?'

Joyce nods. 'That's right. I was here for a while until...' She looks wary and stops. 'Until I wasn't needed any more. And you're right that I've never met you, although I heard later that Lilian was living with her granddaughter.'

'Did you know my mother?'

The older woman bristles. 'I've said too much already. What Lilian wants you to know, she'll tell you; it's not up to me to speak about other people's business, especially an employer who's been so good to me.'

Nell curls her fingers in frustration. There has to be somebody who knows about her mother and, more importantly, is willing to talk about her.

She nods. 'Come into the kitchen. I'll make some tea.'

'I've come to do a job, love, not sit around drinking tea. Besides, I need to check with Adam that you're meant to be here.' She opens a cupboard under the stairs and takes out a red plastic bucket with cleaning implements inside. 'I'll try and get hold of him.'

Nell puts the kettle on and finds an old teapot.

'I'm making a pot anyway, so if you change your mind...' Nell doesn't want tea, but she has to convince Joyce she is who she says she is and get her on side.

Joyce puts on an overall and takes a mobile out of her pocket. She goes out into the hall and Nell hears her talking, presumably to Adam. She wonders what he'll say about her, given that they've barely met. She's already got Joyce down as an overactive busybody who likes her t's to be crossed and her i's dotted.

'Right you are,' she says, coming back into the room and sliding her mobile back into her pocket. 'Adam's told me everything.' Nell stops herself from rolling her eyes. 'It's a good job I did ring him, as

I've been able to do you a favour too. He wasn't too sure whether you really were Lilian's granddaughter and I was able to reassure him on that front. Well, that she does have a granddaughter who would be about your age. Got to be very careful about scams these days, but you won't fool me easily. I'm not one of those gullible old dears you read about being conned out of their life savings, oh no. I may look my age but I've got my wits about me. I can find my way around the Internet as good as any youngster. And I'll have that tea now, if you don't mind. I can take ten minutes before I start work. Adam said he won't be back before six and I fit in my hours as it suits me. He also told me to give you his mobile number.' She scribbles it down on a piece of paper. 'In case you need it.'

Nell pours her a cup of tea and drinks her own leaning against the kitchen counter. Something about Joyce makes her feel on edge. Her eyes are small and brown and constantly darting about as she talks. Her wiry arms look strong, and Nell believes her when she says she can look after herself. 'All this is as much a surprise to you as it is to me.' Nell waves her arm to indicate the house. 'I'd never heard of Adam before, but he tells me he's Lilian's great-nephew.'

'That's right. His mother is Lilian's niece. They've not been in touch for very long. If you know anything about your grandmother, you'll know how self-sufficient she is. Up until the last few years her health has been excellent, but she's elderly now and this is a big house to maintain. She wanted me to move in, but I've got my own family to look after. I come in at least twice a week as it is and do a lot more than the cleaning I'm supposed to. But I could see she wasn't coping on her own. It made her more bitter, if anything. When I gave her an ultimatum, she agreed that I could contact a member of her family. I assumed it would be you, actually, being her next of kin, but she was adamant that it was to be her niece.

'Denise was surprised to hear from Lilian out of the blue, I can tell you. She came over, and between them they agreed this plan for Adam to convert the ground floor for her. Adam's partner has been helping out too. Denise found Lilian some sheltered accommodation to move into temporarily, and Adam's living here to keep an eye on the place while he completes the work. She hasn't spent much money on it over the years and she refuses to sell, but if that's what she wants to do, then it's up to her. She's got her own flat for now and there are people on hand to look after her and activities going on should she want them.'

They exchange a glance for the first time, both acknowledging how unlikely it is that Lilian will want to take part in a communal bingo session or a quiz.

'I'm relieved.' Nell puts her cup in the sink. 'Can you give me the address?'

'Has Adam not done so?'

Nell shakes her head.

'Then it must be for a reason. I'm sure he'll give you it when he's ready.'

Nell swallows down her frustration. At least she knows Adam is genuine and her grandmother is being looked after. She's unsure how she feels about Lilian being vulnerable. And she's trying to ignore the twinge of guilt she feels at not being there for her, until she remembers her mother, who is always lurking at the edge of her mind and lodged in the locket over her heart, and knows she has nothing to reproach herself for.

Joyce looks at her watch and drains her cup, putting it down forcefully on the table. 'Right, enough chat, time to get on with my job. I'll start with the bedrooms. Which room are you in?'

'The one next to Lilian's room. My old bedroom. Were you here earlier today?' With Joyce's unexpected arrival she had forgotten her suspicions about someone being in her room.

Joyce looks puzzled. 'No, you saw me arrive. Do you want me to clean in there?'

'No, you're fine, thanks.' It must have been Adam. What could he have been up to?

*

By the time Joyce comes back downstairs, Nell is looking at the rudiments of the family tree she began at the library. At the moment, all she has are the names of her parents, her four grandparents and Glenys and Denise.

'I don't suppose you know any of the family history, do you?' she asks. 'You've known Lilian so long after all. She must really appreciate you.' She thinks she stands more of a chance of getting on Joyce's good side than Adam's.

'No,' Joyce says, 'not off the top of my head at least. Anyway, I've got news for you. Adam just called. He's spoken to Lilian and she's given you the go-ahead for a visit. He must have caught her at a good moment.'

Or a bad one, thinks Nell. Her grandmother might be just waiting to dig her claws into her after all this time.

'She's in Sunnydale Lodges, out over Bumbles Heath way. Buses don't run that regularly either, if you haven't got a car.' Joyce is searching for something in her pocket as she's talking.

'I haven't. But I've come all this way. I'll get a cab if necessary.'

'Suit yourself. My mobile number is up on the kitchen notice-board in case you need it.'

Nell checks her purse for change.

'Don't look so worried.' Joyce collects her handbag from the kitchen table and takes out a pack of tissues and blows her nose.

Nell sighs. 'My relationship with Grandma hasn't been easy. You must know what she's like.'

'She's my employer, I don't comment on her behaviour.'

'Fair enough,' Nell says, but she wishes the woman would lighten up.

'What brings you back here then, if you're not on speaking terms?'

'My mother,' Nell says, and Joyce stares at her before closing her bag with an emphatic snap.

CHAPTER TEN

After tracking down a Wi-Fi code, which she eventually finds pinned on the noticeboard, and a frustrating search on the Internet, Nell establishes that the bus she needs runs once an hour, and if she leaves quickly she can make the next one.

Forty minutes later, she steps out at Bumbles Heath. The bus stops in front of a bakery, and the smell of coffee drifts out as she looks around her to get her bearings.

'I'm so pleased you're still open,' she says to the baker, a rotund man with a white apron stretched over his stomach and a friendly smile.

'Only just. What can I get you? Everything's half price in the last hour.'

She buys a sandwich and a hot drink, as she hasn't had any lunch. 'Do you know how I can get to Sunnydale Lodges?'

'Ah yes, that's easy enough from here. Cross the street and follow the road around to the left. And if you want a nice spot to eat your sandwich first, there's a bench just under the trees over there.'

'Thanks,' says Nell. 'I will. It's a nice afternoon.'

'Make the most of it,' he says, 'I doubt we'll get many more now autumn is setting in.'

She crosses over to the bench and takes her time over her drink and sandwich, aware that she's putting off the inevitable, psyching herself up to face her grandmother, the guilt she always feels.

*

Sunnydale Lodges consists of a crescent of modern bungalows. Nell heads to reception to introduce herself, and the receptionist tells her that Lilian is in bungalow number 14.

'How is she?' she asks, hoping the woman will say that her grandmother has had a personality transplant.

'She's doing well, considering.'

'Considering?'

The woman looks wary. 'Have you not spoken to her for a while?'

'No,' Nell says, 'but she's expecting me.'

The woman pinches her lips together.

'I'll let her tell you,' she says.

Nell feels another layer of worry pile on top of everything else as she heads to number 14, dragging her feet now she's finally here. The sandwich she so enjoyed earlier is lodged in her stomach like a rock. She drinks some water from the bottle she carries with her, then straightens herself and rings the doorbell.

A few long moments drag by, during which she is torn between hoping the door remains closed and the need to get answers to her questions. Eventually a shape appears in the glass panel. Nell barely recognises the small figure shuffling towards her, remembering only a tall woman dressed in severe clothing. The door pulls back with a grating squeal and Nell is face to face with her grandmother.

Lilian might be reduced in stature, but her face is as she remembers, albeit carved with lines, criss-crossing from her eyes and around her mouth. She hasn't lost the habit of tilting her chin upwards so that she appears to look down over her strong Roman nose.

'I heard you were back,' she says, and only now does Nell notice the ornate cane she leans on with her left hand. Lilian wobbles slightly, quickly pulling herself upright. The duck's head on the cane stares at Nell with its beady eye.

Still maintaining standards, Nell thinks, instinctively drawing back her shoulders and standing tall. Lilian gives her a quick once-over, a flicker of surprise in her eyes, swiftly extinguished.

'I suppose you'd better come in.' She turns and walks slowly down a narrow corridor and into a room on the left, resting the walking stick against the wall as she lowers herself onto a red velvet sofa. Nell waits in the doorway, the shock of seeing her grandmother temporarily paralysing her.

'Come in and sit down, for goodness' sake,' Lilian says, waving her bony hand at an armchair opposite.

Nell takes in the neat room: red curtains to match the carpet and sofa, a chunky television in the corner and a small table to the left of the sofa, on which stands a glass of water and a couple of magazines, a copy of a daily newspaper.

She shuffles out of her coat and perches on the armchair. She maintains a calm, relaxed pose, even though inside she is in turmoil. Only a few minutes back in the presence of this woman who, once upon a time, she felt strongly enough about to run away from, and she's quaking at that voice, that face that has so much power over her. She imagines herself into a work scenario, standing in front of a roomful of people listening with interest to what she has to say, and feels her confidence return.

'You've met Adam, then.' Nell is grateful for this line of enquiry, although she has more pressing matters to discuss. This is safer – she can't afford to rush in and be thrown out without the answers she has come for. Lilian is like an instrument that needs careful playing.

'Yes. It's good you're back in touch with Denise. Joyce told me.'

'Ah yes, Joyce.'

'Is she the same Joyce who used to clean for you?'

'She is. I found myself needing help again, and before advertising, I made enquiries to see if she would be interested. It saved me the bother of interviewing, never mind letting a stranger into my home.' She visibly shudders. 'She can keep an eye on Adam too; after all, I haven't known him long, although he has been useful.'

'He wasn't very friendly.'

'And do you blame him?'

Nell feels a rush of blood to her head. If she was a cat, her tail would be swishing in the air, giving a feline flick of fury. But she shakes her head, imagining a zip over her mouth, only letting the most carefully prepared words slip out.

'Why is it you've come back?' Lilian asks, her eyes seeking out Nell's. Nell returns the gaze, her strength returning as she thinks of the woman whose image she carries around her neck, close to her heart. 'I suppose you heard I was ill. Is that it, is that why you're suddenly so eager to see me?'

So this is what the woman at the reception must have been referring to.

'No, I didn't know that. What's wrong?' Nell notices how pale her grandmother's face is, and how frail she looks, though she'd put that down to ageing.

'The dreaded cancer. Gets most of us in the end.' Lilian straightens herself, and again there's a glimpse of the woman she was before. 'It's treatable, so they tell me. An operation, then chemotherapy. *If* I want to go through with it. I have a choice, they've made that clear.'

'You'll have it, won't you?'

'Do you care?' Lilian asks. 'You haven't exactly been the doting granddaughter, have you? What is it that brings you back here?'

'You haven't heard, then?' Nell says, tilting her head to one side in deliberate provocation.

The slightest glimmer of a frown creases the old lady's already crinkled forehead.

'Heard?' She too cocks her head, mirroring Nell, each assuming their familiar battle position.

'My mother is dead,' Nell says. She's rehearsed this line and is confident she won't let the tears burst forth; not here, she won't give Lilian the satisfaction. She is strong for Sarah, who no longer has a voice. 'She died last month. I was called to a reading of her will. It was very interesting.'

She holds her grandmother's stare. Lilian looks away. Nell waits. The silence is thick between them.

'Aren't you going to say anything?'

'What would you like me to say?'

It occurs to her that her grandmother might not be ill at all, but feigning this illness so that she can get away with not answering her questions. But Lilian's skin has a grey pallor, her limbs are skeletal, the skin stretched over her claw-like hands.

'You told me she was dead.' Nell's voice shakes and she gets to her feet. She's overcome with an urge to scratch at her skin, to remove this itchy feeling that has taken over her body since learning about her mother.

'It was better that way.'

'For you?'

Lilian blinks slowly, like a reptile, before answering.

'For you, for me, for both of us.'

'Tell me.' Nell controls her voice, although she wants to take Lilian by her bony shoulders and shake her until she reveals everything, no matter how painful it is to hear. Anything would be better than this shard of ice that is lodged in her heart. 'Please,' she adds, clutching her hands together to stop herself letting the rage out and ruining her chances of finding out what she so desperately wants to know.

'I refuse to elaborate.' Despite her frailty, Lilian's jaw is lifted and her eyes blaze at Nell, daring her to challenge her.

Nell is transported back to her younger self sitting in front of a table one parents' evening in the cavernous school hall, conversations in hushed voices taking place all around. A teacher made a suggestion Lilian wasn't happy with. Nell can't remember what it was, but she will never forget the way her grandmother's voice rang out through the hall, so that conversations stalled and heads were raised, curious children turning to stare at Nell, already an outsider on account of where she lived. Nell understood that her grandmother had her best interests at heart, but the way she went about it made her cringe. The friends she'd made were precious and she didn't want to lose them.

She tries to relax her posture, to appear less confrontational. Lilian will always win a fight. She softens her voice.

'It was such a shock, Gran.' The word feels alien on her tongue. 'When I received the call from the solicitor, my whole world turned upside down. She'd been living in the same city as me; maybe our paths had crossed and I would never have known. The solicitor tells me you've been paying her rent for years, so you must have cared for her.' Lilian's face remains impassive. 'I have so many questions.'

'Whereas I have only one. Why did you leave?'

'Because I was an impulsive teenager. This town is so small and my friends were all far away, and you know what the bus service is like. I'm sorry I hurt you, really I am. I should have waited until I was eighteen, but we had that stupid row about my career, and you know how hot-headed I was. But it worked out OK. I've built up a good life for myself. It's not too late for us, but we have to be straight with one another, don't you see?'

Lilian is gazing towards the window, chin raised, but her face has softened.

'Perhaps it's time I told you a few things.'

Nell grips the arms of the chair.

CHAPTER ELEVEN

'I'm sorry you had to find out about your mother the way you did. Obviously it's come as a shock to you. I'll cover any funeral expenses, naturally.'

Nell lets go of the chair. 'It's not about money. Why didn't you tell me? I asked you so many times, and you made it clear the subject was off limits. Even about my dad, you were so vague.'

'Because it wasn't good for you to dwell on what happened, and it was too painful for me to talk about. It wouldn't have been healthy for you to know too much about it.'

And the truth. But Nell doesn't say this aloud, not wanting to antagonise her grandmother when she's finally about to talk. Besides, she has a point. Everything she knows about her parents is forever imprinted in her memory.

'Before I tell you this, I want you to be sure you really want to know. I won't be able to unsay the words. There are things about your mother that I believed it best to spare you. If you insist on knowing the truth, then so be it.'

'Of course I want the truth. My mother has always been a mystery to me. I want to know everything I can about her. What have I got to lose?' Nell worries at a split fingernail. The truth is, she's terrified. What if her mother isn't the person she has built her up to be? She feels for the locket under her jumper, seeking comfort.

'Very well.' Lilian sips at a glass of water. 'You have to understand, when your father died, it was a terrible time, the most awful shock for both of us. Sarah, of course, was devastated. They hadn't been married long, and that day she had found out she was pregnant. They were going out to dinner and she'd planned to tell him that evening. Sadly, she never got to do so, and he died not knowing he was to be a father.'

Nell gasps. 'Pregnant? You mean…?' She drops her head into her hands, her pulse rapid. 'You lied to me, you said I was a small child. This means I was in the crash too.'

Lilian looks at her and her eyes contain a softness Nell hasn't seen before.

'Sarah went to pieces, and I did all I could to look after her. I believe now she may have been suffering from post-natal depression, as she seemed unable to care for you; indeed, at times I wasn't sure she remembered that she even had you. But she got better slowly, and started to live her life again; she went back to work part-time. After a while, though, I began to lose patience. She was neglectful of you, and careless. There were a series of incidents; I don't need to go into the details, but suffice to say I was beginning to realise she was unfit to look after you.

'I tried everything, talking to her and reminding her that you were the only living link to David, whom she'd loved so much, as I did. Things came to a head when she was looking after you one night and she fell asleep and knocked a hot drink over. You were burned.' She stares at Nell, who can't help but seize her lower arm. 'Yes, that was how that blemish really came about. Another thing I couldn't bear to tell you. But do you understand now? How could I tell you what a terrible mother you had, neglecting you so badly that you came to harm? It would have destroyed the image you had of her. All I ever wanted was to keep you safe.'

Nell opens her mouth, but she's lost for words. A memory she's never forgotten. She'd fallen on her arm and was at the hospital with her grandmother, yet it isn't the pain she remembers – though it must have hurt – but the comments a nurse made when Lilian had gone to speak to the doctor. They are as ingrained in her mind as the mark is on her skin.

'Nasty burn you've got there,' the woman said as she eased Nell's arm into the X-ray machine.

'It's a birthmark,' Nell said, hating having to expose her arm in this way.

'Who told you that?' the nurse asked.

'Grandma.'

Nell heard raised voices when the nurse took her grandmother aside, and she had to wait ages after that and didn't see the nurse again. She tried to ask Lilian about the mark, but her grandmother dismissed her fears as nonsense, saying the nurse was a trainee and didn't know what she was talking about. Lilian had such an authoritative air about her and people listened when she spoke, wherever she went. She was the sort of person you'd stop to ask directions from, knowing you were in capable hands. She told Nell to banish 'that nonsense' from her mind, so Nell did. Until now, when she knows the truth.

'Before the accident, I had given her an ultimatum. Either she had to change and take responsibility for the fact that she had a child or I would report her. That night was the catalyst. Her actions had caused you actual bodily harm and she left me with no choice. I called social services. These things drag on and I was at my wits' end. Eventually I offered to take care of you, but on the condition that Sarah left until she was well enough to return. Sadly, that day never came.'

'But she was ill, she needed help.'

'Don't you think I don't know that?' Lilian's eyes flash and some of her old vigour returns. 'This had gone on for months and I'd tried everything. I felt it was kinder to let you believe your mother had died with your father and you'd come into my custody that way.'

'But why did you never talk about her? I have no idea what she was like. I'd never even seen a photograph of her.' Nell doesn't want Lilian to know about her precious necklace; that is between her and her mother, a secret that only they share.

'The experience took a terrible toll on me too. Don't forget I was grieving for my only son, as well as trying to look after Sarah and the demands of a small baby. Joyce was no longer around, as she had her own family to contend with – it really was the most trying time of my life. And you weren't an easy baby. But never accuse me of not loving you.'

Of course she would have been a disturbed child given the traumatic events of her short life. She feels a pang of pain for her younger self, the tragic circumstances of her birth and never having known her father. And she sees her grandmother through the eyes of an adult – what an impossible situation Lilian was in.

'It must have been so hard for you.'

Lilian places her hand on Nell's. Her skin feels cold.

'But did you never think about how I would feel if I found out?'

'I prayed that day would never come. If your mother chose to come back then I would deal with it, but I was confident that she wouldn't.'

'How were you so confident?'

Lilian makes a dismissive gesture with her hand. The large diamond of her engagement ring catches the light.

'It wasn't in your best interests and she knew that.'

The doorbell rings, startling Nell, and Lilian drops her hand to glance at her watch.

'That will be the nurse,' she says. 'Four times a day somebody turns up to attend to me. So degrading. Would you mind letting her in?'

The nurse is a tired-looking woman in a smart uniform.

'Hello,' she says. 'I didn't realise Lilian would have company.'

Lilian appears at the living-room door.

'Come in, Sandra. Nell is just leaving.'

Sandra smiles at Nell and steps into the hallway.

'Thank you for visiting,' Lilian says, and Nell reluctantly picks up her jacket. 'Adam tells me you want to stay in the house.'

'Is that OK?'

'Of course. You're my granddaughter.'

CHAPTER TWELVE

1991

'Sarah.' Lilian's strident voice booms up the stairs and Sarah lets out a long breath, willing herself to stay calm. Merely the thought of Lilian these days is enough to make her heart beat a little faster and her hands to sweat. But today is different; she has a little secret inside her, another weapon to fight her with, and Lilian can do nothing to claw it away from her. Once David knows about the baby, he'll want to move out as quickly as she does.

Her ultimatum shook him up. The very next morning he slid a casual remark into the conversation about their plans to find their own house in the future. She heard him arguing with his mother later, and that night in bed he held her tight and promised she would always come first in his life. The subject wasn't mentioned in front of Lilian again, but Sarah knows David loves her, and that gives her strength.

It took her three months to find the dream property. This morning Philip from the estate agent's called to ask her if they had made a final decision on the cottage that has filled her mind since the first viewing.

She had taken David there the previous night. She held his hand and led him up to the master bedroom with the view over the cloud of white blossom on the cherry tree in the garden. She showed him the two smaller bedrooms, which would be perfect for a guest room and a nursery, and the smile that split his face in two was infectious. He took her in his arms and spun her round.

'There must have been a day when your parents were in this position,' she said, 'imagining their first home together. And think how many happy years they had. I want the same for us, and you do too, don't you?'

'It's perfect,' he said. 'You're right. Mum's been grieving for long enough. She's become too dependent on us.'

'She has.'

'We'd be doing her a favour by moving out. I'm so sorry, Sarah, I've been so wrapped up with my studies and left you to sort all this out by yourself.'

'I don't mind, as long as we tell her.'

'This weekend, I promise.'

And now she has the baby to tell him about too.

'Sarah.' Lilian's voice is closer now.

'Coming,' she calls, and jumps off the bed, not wanting her mother-in-law to intrude into her room, where she's been going through the Yellow Pages and making a list of nurseries. She runs down the stairs, smoothing her jumper down over her still flat stomach, and smiles to herself before entering the living room.

'What time will you be back for dinner tonight?'

Sarah bites her lip to stop herself from smirking. She wondered how long it would take her mother-in-law to complain about her being late for dinner twice this week. She can't help rebelling now she knows escape is on the horizon.

'Actually, we won't be here for dinner. We're going out for a meal.'

'David didn't mention it,' Lilian says, pursing her thin lips, her red lipstick bleeding into the tiny cracks around her mouth, the colour incongruous against her severe black dress. 'Are you sure?'

He doesn't know yet, that's why. Sarah keeps this thought to herself.

'Of course I'm sure.'

She'll call David and insist he meets her this evening. She'll take him to their favourite restaurant, where she can tell him her news, and later they can inform Lilian that they've found a property and will be moving out. No need to wait for the weekend as they agreed. She'll ask Philip to make it happen as soon as possible. No child of hers will be born into this house with Lilian and her strict rules. Sarah has so much love to give – she wants to make up for her own motherless childhood and make sure her baby has two loving parents.

'Do you have to go out? It's very short notice. I've already made preparations and I find it quite irresponsible of you. I look forward to our meals together.'

Sarah wishes she could tell her how much she hates them. Sitting around the small table at seven o'clock precisely, Lilian holding court. Mealtime conversation revolves around Lilian asking David questions about his day and ignoring Sarah. David has challenged his mother about this; of course she denied it, blaming Sarah's oversensitivity. These thoughts give rise to the rush of familiar anger and she can't help brushing her hand against her stomach, reminding herself to keep calm. She makes a point of smoothing her sleeves too in case Lilian's watchful eyes notice the movement and make assumptions. She'll insist David doesn't tell her until at least three months are up, and by then they'll hopefully be in their own place and Lilian's apron strings will be severed.

'We do have to go out,' Sarah says. 'And why wouldn't we? It's a Friday night and that's what normal couples do.'

Lilian frowns, and makes a mental note to speak to David about Sarah's insolence towards her. Another late night waiting up for them to get home; she can't help but worry when David is out.

'David and I have always watched a film on a Friday night, it's a family tradition.'

Sarah wonders how Gerald used to feel about this, and whether he felt as excluded as she does. She wishes she could have asked him.

The sound of a key in the front door lock cuts through the chill between them, and the familiar sounds of Joyce arriving gives them both another focus. Lilian takes the cleaner through to the kitchen, and Sarah escapes upstairs and lies on her bed, listening to the murmur of voices drifting through the ceiling, Lilian's strident tones issuing commands, with Joyce's higher-pitched voice making the occasional interjection. Sarah has been tempted to confide in Joyce as the only other outsider in this house, but Joyce is fiercely loyal to Lilian and she daren't trust her.

She thinks back to this morning in the bathroom. After waiting until David had left, she locked herself in their en suite, taking no chances while she took the most important test of her life so far. Waiting for the thin blue line to appear took forever, and she counted the tiles in the bathroom over and over while she waited, forgetting the total the minute the result came through. She stashed the stick in a make-up pouch inside her handbag, to be revealed later over their candlelit dinner.

The murmur of voices continues downstairs, and she picks up the phone extension and dials David's college. She leaves a message for David to ring her. She'll make sure she gets to the phone before Lilian does; that way her mother-in-law won't be able to scupper her plans.

Sarah spends the afternoon in the living room reading. Lilian is out, so she's able to relax. Her mother-in-law's disapproving looks make her feel uncomfortable and on edge. In the beginning, she'd attempt to engage her in conversation, but the chilly reception and the way Lilian closed down the interaction soon stopped her even trying. The living room is cosy, and reading makes Sarah's eyes heavy. She must have dozed off, because the next minute she hears Lilian's voice answering the phone.

'Sarah?' Lilian always pronounces her name as if it's something distasteful she's extracting from a plughole. 'Yes, I believe she's home. Who should I say is asking?'

Sarah feels a griping motion in her stomach, fearful that it may be Philip on the phone, as it's clearly not David. She's already on her feet and moving into the hall, but she's too late. Lilian holds the phone at arm's length, as if it's on fire, and Sarah attempts to smile, then turns away from her and coils the telephone wire around her fingers.

She barely says a word as Philip tells her another couple have made an offer on the cottage and he needs an answer today. She promises to call him back and takes her time placing the avocado-green receiver back in its holder, Lilian's eyes drilling into her back.

'Why would an estate agent be calling you?' Lilian asks, folding her arms. At that moment, Joyce appears.

'Mrs Wetherby, come quickly, I've had an accident.'

Sarah sends up a silent prayer, then jumps when the phone rings again. It's David, and he hasn't got long as he's between lectures. She tells him she's booked a table at Frederico's this evening. She looks over her shoulder as she tells him Lilian is fine with it, and arranges to meet him there.

Sarah pauses before going into the kitchen, feeling self-conscious in her little black dress, but her throat is dry and she's desperate for a glass of water. Besides, much as she doesn't want to, she'll have to check with Lilian whether it's OK to take the car. If she refuses, she'll have to call a taxi, but as she won't be drinking, she might as well drive. She takes a deep breath and pushes open the door.

'Don't you look lovely?' Joyce says. A box of plasters lies next to her on the counter.

Lilian looks her up and down with her small birdlike eyes.

'You'll get cold in that,' she says. 'Is David coming home first?'

'No, he's meeting me in town. Do you mind if I borrow the car?'

Lilian stares at her for what seems like an interminable amount of time. 'I suppose not,' she says. 'I'll have to remove my bags from the boot. I haven't unpacked from my visit to town earlier.'

'I can do that for you,' Joyce says.

'No.' Lilian's tone is unexpectedly harsh. 'I'm quite capable of looking after myself, thank you. Seems like I'll have to start getting used to it.'

Sarah wonders how much Lilian gleaned from the estate agent earlier, but better that than the inquisition she was expecting. She pours herself a glass of cold water. Joyce is putting dishes away.

'Off to Frederico's again, are you?'

Sarah smiles. 'Yes, it's our favourite. I thought she'd say no to me borrowing the car and make me get a taxi.'

Joyce closes the cupboard door and hangs up the tea towel. 'Try not to take it personally. If it's any consolation, she was the same way with David's previous girlfriend – and she didn't last long. You and David are perfect for one another, anyone can see that. It's just taking Lilian a while to adjust.'

'Did she say anything to you about the phone call earlier?' Sarah doesn't want to give too much away, but Joyce is her only conduit into Lilian's psyche.

'No. Was it important? I cut my finger and she helped me put on a plaster.'

Sarah takes her water into the sitting room and switches the television on to watch the news. She'll have to leave in five minutes. She finishes her drink and takes the glass back into the kitchen before getting her coat. Lilian comes in through the front door and hands her the car keys.

'Thanks,' she says.

'Don't think I've forgotten the phone call you received earlier. Does David know what you're up to?'

'Of course he does. David is my husband. He's been waiting for the right moment to tell you. We want our own place. Please don't take it personally; we aren't rejecting you – of course you'll always be welcome.' The car keys dig into Sarah's hand as she clutches them tightly. If she had her way, Lilian would never set foot in their new house.

'This is David's home.' Lilian hisses the words into Sarah's face, making her recoil in shock. 'How dare you try and take him away from me. I want you to call the agent and tell him there's been a mistake. Otherwise I will.'

Sarah gasps and steps back, hoping Lilian won't notice her hands shaking. The way the woman looks down her beaky nose with venom in her eyes makes Sarah feel like a sparrow caught by a bird of prey.

Outside, the wind ruffles her neatly arranged hair and she rushes towards the car, which is parked in the front drive. She glances back to see if Lilian is following her, but she's standing in the doorway, stiff and threatening, like a security guard. Sarah fumbles with the car keys and drops them on the ground. Eventually she manages to unlock the car and gets into the driving seat just as a vehicle pulls up in the street outside.

'Sarah.' David's voice is so unexpected, tears spring into her eyes. He's leaning into a taxi and paying the driver. Has Lilian got to him and told him not to go to the restaurant?

'What are you doing here?' she asks. 'We're supposed to be meeting at Frederico's.'

He shifts his backpack onto his shoulder. 'Gerry was getting a taxi so I thought I might as well come with him. I'll just drop my bag into the house…'

'No,' she says, 'please, I'll explain when we get there. We have to go now. Put your bag in the car.'

David frowns, glancing up to see his mother in the porch. He waves at her and throws his bag onto the back seat.

'You drive,' Sarah says, shuffling across to the passenger seat; she's in no state to concentrate. Lilian's threats are racing round her head.

David gets into the driving seat and starts the car. Sarah glances in the rear-view mirror and sees Lilian running towards the car, waving her arms as if to stop them. She winds down her window and sticks her hand out, waving back, wishing she were brave enough to give her the V sign, then slides the window shut with a satisfying click and looks straight ahead. It feels like a small triumph.

David accelerates out of the drive, oblivious to his mother's agitation. The car picks up speed as it travels down the road and she wishes he wouldn't drive so fast and then the car is sliding and the cry he makes is like no sound Sarah has ever heard as the steering wheel veers out of control and the car is turning and turning and blackness descends.

CHAPTER THIRTEEN
2019

Nell sits on the edge of her bed and switches on the bedside lamp. The light is dim and shines into the corner of the room where her unpacked rucksack sits. This day has stretched out like a rubber band and her head is pounding. Adam was up in his room when she got back and she was glad not to have to make conversation. Her grandmother's comments about her mother have shattered her illusions. Never have the characters she has created for her mother included somebody who would cause her harm. Yet it would explain why her grandmother was always so protective of her, and Nell is overcome with a wave of sadness and guilt that she chose to break away from that.

Next morning Adam is nowhere to be seen, although he's left a half-eaten bowl of cereal on the table. Nell has just sat down with a cup of coffee when she hears someone coming in the front door.

'Hello,' Joyce says as she bustles into the kitchen with two shopping bags. She drops them on the table, making Nell's coffee splash from the cup. She picks it up. Joyce is wearing a hooded blue anorak covering her cleaning apron, and sensible shoes. She unpacks the cleaning materials she's bought and puts them into a cupboard.

'I wasn't expecting so see you again so soon,' Nell says.

'It's not my regular day, but Adam asked me to come in.'

'To keep an eye on me, you mean. Honestly, there's no need. I'm hardly going to nick my grandmother's stuff, and I'm a lot tidier than he is. Does he expect you to clear up after him?' She indicates the draining rack.

'He's usually very tidy for a man. He must have been in a hurry.'

Nell frowns. Is he trying to provoke her?

'Did you find Sunnydale Lodges OK?' Joyce asks.

'Yes thanks, although it was bit of a shock to find out she's got cancer.'

'It's treatable. She'll be fine. Lilian is as tough as old boots.'

Joyce goes into the utility room off the kitchen and comes back with the hoover.

'Can I ask you something?'

'You can try me.' She sets the hoover on the floor.

'Did you know my father?'

'Oh yes, David, such a tragedy. I was here when he first… You know he was adopted, don't you?'

Nell nods.

'That's a relief. I didn't want to shock you. That's what made it all so terrible.'

'I don't understand.'

'The accident. Lilian had chosen him, you see; he was special. I've never seen anyone so devoted to a child, almost too devoted, to the point where it wasn't good for either of them. That became evident when he died. Lilian went to pieces. She dismissed me then, you know. She had a breakdown, reading between the lines.'

'How did the adoption come about?'

Joyce glances at the clock.

'Please,' Nell says. 'This is important. I have so many questions and there's only so much I can find out in documents, and Adam won't tell me anything.'

Joyce shakes her head. 'He won't know anything. I've already told you, he's only hooked up with Lilian recently. Knows where his bread's buttered, that's what I'm thinking.' She narrows her eyes. 'Call me cynical, but all these relatives cropping up suddenly when Lilian's health isn't so good makes me highly suspicious. Frail old lady owning a magnificent house such as this, and no children. He's made no secret of the fact that he's hard up and he's got small children. I'm not surprised he hasn't welcomed you with open arms. I'm amazed he's let you stay here at all.'

'I'm not the slightest bit interested in all this.' Nell gestures at her surroundings. 'I don't exactly have happy memories of the place. All I want is to find out what happened to my mother. Can you imagine what it's like to find out that the mother you'd believed to be dead all your life was actually alive and well, but by the time you've found out it's too late?' Tears well in her eyes and she bats them away furiously. Crying about it won't get her anywhere, and Joyce isn't the type to sympathise with her. She's like Lilian in that respect – probably why she's stuck by her when nobody else would. 'Lilian's given me her version of events, but I have no idea whether she's telling me the truth or not.' Her voice is getting louder and she takes a breath before she says, 'So please, if you know anything, please tell me. It won't go any further, it's just for me.'

'What do you want to know exactly? Like I said, I was suddenly let go right when she needed me most, but I couldn't make her see sense.'

'Tell me about that time.'

Joyce sighs. 'I suppose it won't do any harm now she knows you're here. Lilian had always wanted children. She used to be far more relaxed when she was younger. She was devoted to Gerald and she used to talk about when they'd start a family; she even referred to the smaller guest bedroom as the nursery. She was used to getting what she wanted, and not getting pregnant wasn't something she'd expected to happen. After two years of trying, with no result, she stopped talking about it, and relations between her and Mr Wetherby were somewhat strained. My guess – and that's all it is, as she wouldn't talk about anything personal any more with me – is that she suspected Gerald was the one with the problem and it diminished him in her eyes. I know there were lots of doctor's appointments; they used to always do things like that together.

'Over time, she gradually withdrew. She even stopped seeing her friends. One of her closest female friends was expecting, and Lilian shunned her. It was quite unexpected – these were close friends I'm talking about; they'd been on holiday together and everything.

'Things went quiet for a bit, and I assumed they'd given up, when one day she announces that they're going through the adoption procedure. Next thing I know she's all smiles, and off they go one afternoon and come back with David. They say you shouldn't try and have a child to seal a bad relationship, but in their case it was the best thing that could have happened to them. "I chose him, Joyce," she used to say to me, "which means he's more wanted than a natural child. I'll never let anyone harm him." She must have been grateful to him too, for bringing her and Gerald back together. They weren't lovey-dovey like they used to be back in the beginning – she'd become much harder and she never lost that – but they patched things up for the sake of the child. And he was a lovely little boy, adorable, so well behaved and such a cute face. I told her then he was going to grow up to be a right little heartbreaker and joked about her wanting the right girl for him, but she didn't like that, not one bit, and I knew then that she was going to find it very difficult when he started dating. No girl was ever going to be good enough for her David.'

'So do you remember when he first met my mum, Sarah?'

She nods. 'Oh yes, she was his first serious girlfriend, serious enough to get past Lilian, I mean. He'd dated a couple of girls before that, but she frightened them off. It was the first time I'd ever known them row, him and his mum. Sarah was a lovely girl and she got on extremely well with Gerald, which didn't go unnoticed by Lilian, and the two of them started bickering again. David was out at work all day so he was unaware of it, as they were careful not to row in front of him. Lilian was very much about appearances, so anything that was happening in her family was kept very much at home. That's why she trusted me, because I never discussed what went on here with anyone. That's when she promised to see me right.'

'What do you mean?'

'She always paid me very generously, even when I was sick, and there's not many employers that would treat a cleaner as a friend.' She looks at her watch and sighs. 'Now, nice as it is to reminisce, I have work to do.'

'Is there anything I can do to help?' Nell doesn't want Joyce to stop – she's desperate to find out everything she can about her mother. She sighs when Joyce tells her no and takes the hoover upstairs.

The noise of the appliance is loud and she almost misses the knock at the door. She dashes into the hall and opens the front door, but there's no sign of anyone. As she steps forward to look around the corner, in case whoever it was has gone to the side entrance, her foot lands on something squishy. She recoils in horror, looking down to see a bundle of tissue paper with what look like bloodstains on it, tied up with string. She holds her breath as she pokes it with her foot. A patch of grey fur and a pink tail reveal a dead mouse. Not a present from the cat, but a deliberate delivery.

She runs to the bottom of the drive and scans the street, but there's no sign of anybody. She goes back into the house to get a dustpan and brush, but first she'll take a photograph as proof to show Adam.

The whine of the hoover ceases and Joyce appears at the top of the stairs.

'Why is the front door open? You look as if you've seen a ghost.'

'Come and see.' Nell points to the mouse and Joyce gives a little shriek.

'That cat is a nuisance.'

'It wasn't the cat. It was wrapped up, look.' She indicates the paper and string, smeared pink with blood.

'Who would do such a thing?'

'I wish I knew. Somebody who doesn't want me here, obviously.'

'You don't know that. It might be meant for Adam.'

'Has something like this happened before?'

'Not that I know of.'

'Hardly anyone knows I'm here apart from him and the solicitor.'

'Be careful,' Joyce says. 'I don't trust that young man.'

'Why would you say that?'

'It's like I said before. Ageing aunt living on her own in a huge house; he turns up offering to help and moves in. Tenants have rights these days. That's all I'm saying.'

What Joyce isn't saying is that she thinks Nell has turned up for the exact same reason.

CHAPTER FOURTEEN

After the incident with the mouse, Nell has to get out of the house. She shouts goodbye to Joyce but doubts she can hear her over the sound of the hoover. She just makes the bus, running to catch up with it as it arrives at the stop.

Jenny is the first person she sees on entering the library. Her red hair is loose today, and she is chatting to a woman at the desk. She spots Nell and gives her a bright smile.

'Thank you so much,' the woman says, taking two books from the counter and putting them in her bag. 'I'll let you know what I think when I return them.'

'Hi,' Jenny says. 'I was hoping you'd be back. How's the family research going?'

'Slowly,' Nell says. 'I'm going to do some more today up in the reference library, but I was wondering whether you had a break coming up. We could get that coffee.'

Jenny glances at her watch. 'Oh lovely, thank you. I've got a half-hour break in fifteen minutes.'

'Great. I'll have a look around the library while I wait.'

Half an hour later, they are ensconced in a café.

'They do the best coffee in town here,' Jenny says. 'Not that there's a great deal of competition.'

Nell laughs. 'I'm spoilt for choice in London. You can't move for coffee bars, chains, independents, even mobile coffee vans.'

'Tell me all about your life in London,' Jenny says. 'It's been ages since I've met anyone who doesn't come from one of the neighbouring villages. Most of my friends are people I went to school with here.' She laughs. 'I need to get out more.'

Nell tells Jenny about her friends, her flat and her busy job. 'I love living in the city, but my job is so pressured. It's only now that I've had a chance to come here and stop for a while that I realise how much of my time and energy it takes up. And now, finding out about my mother...' She pauses, unsure how much to give away, but Jenny's face is open and friendly, and Nell decides she can trust her. She gives her a short résumé of her current situation, and by the time she gets to the part about the will and her mother, Jenny is open-mouthed and squeals when she mentions the mouse.

'I can't believe this,' she says. 'It's like something off one of those programmes my grandmother watches on daytime television. I totally get why you're researching it. You must be so confused. If there's anything I can do to help, I'd be fascinated, though it won't be like those celebrity programmes where they have hundreds of researchers at their disposal, finding out the most amazing facts. I'm afraid all I can offer is this lowly librarian.' She points to herself. 'You must be angry with your gran.'

'I'm furious she's lied to me, but worried too. I've been imagining her locked up somewhere.'

'It sounds like you've been reading too many crime thrillers,' Jenny says. 'Although the mouse is seriously weird. It makes me shudder just thinking about it.'

'When it arrived this morning, it certainly felt like I was in one. Luckily, there's a cleaner, Joyce, who's been around for ages and she was able to verify his story. I went to see Lilian as soon as I could in her new accommodation; it's not far from here, at Bumbles Heath.'

Jenny nods. 'My gran's friend Muriel has moved there recently; she loves it. She can maintain her independence while at the same time having help on hand if she needs it.'

'It's a nice place.'

'Is Mrs Wetherby planning to sell the house now she's moved out?'

'No, Adam is converting the ground floor for her so that she'll be able to move back. He's quite cagey. I don't know whether he feels threatened by me. It was a shock seeing Lilian; she always used to be such a formidable woman. I felt strangely protective of her and I'm not sure I trust Adam's motives. I hope he isn't taking advantage of her. Joyce has made it clear she thinks he's after her money, and I'm sure he thinks the same of me. I certainly don't want Lilian's house; I just want to get to the truth.'

'Well I'd love to help you,' Jenny says, glancing at her phone. 'Oh, look at the time, I must get back or I'll be in trouble. My boss is a real stickler for timekeeping. But let's do this again. Coffee's on me next time.'

Nell spends the rest of the day in the reference library research-ing her family tree. She finds references to the birth, death and marriage certificates for her parents and grandparents, and can see the connection to Adam's parents, which reassures her that he is genuine. She takes photos of the information – she can show these to Adam along with her driving licence to prove she is who she says she is, just in case he's still having doubts. When she's had enough, she heads downstairs to say goodbye to Jenny.

'See you soon,' she says.

Adam's van isn't in the drive, and she wonders whether he has been to see Lilian today. Next time she gets to speak to her grandmother, she'll make sure she really is happy to have him staying in her house.

She knows something is wrong as soon as she opens the front door. The coats that normally hang on the rack behind the door are strewn on the hall floor, and there's a smell of tobacco in the air. Adam doesn't smoke in the house, as far as she knows. She pulls the door to without closing it and tiptoes further down the hall, peering hesitantly into the front room, which is undisturbed, then checking the lounge, which is also as she left it. It's the same in the kitchen. The back door is secured and the garden is empty.

She goes back to the hall and stands listening for a moment, her pulse thumping. Nothing. She's still holding her keys and grips them between her fingers, a move she learned years ago from a self-defence guru online. The stairs creak under her weight and she pauses before summoning up her courage and taking the last few steps quickly. She wants to get this over with. From her vantage point on the landing, she can see that the bathroom and her grandmother's room are untouched. She crosses through Lilian's room to the en suite bathroom and pauses in front of the dressing table, where a bottle of Yardley English Lavender perfume stands as it stood back when she was a teenager. She can't help lifting the top and smelling the familiar fragrance, and is ambushed by an image of her grandmother catching her doing the very same thing as a child and plucking the bottle from her hands. Nell never went into her bedroom again. She still feels as if she is in forbidden territory, but she's calmer now, as none of the rooms appear to have been disturbed.

But as soon as she steps into her own room, her senses ratchet up into high alert. One of her bras and a pair of knickers are laid out on the bed. Nausea rises in her throat. She drags her eyes from the creepiness. The wardrobe door is open and the clothes have been flung about. Her legs feel unsteady and she sinks onto the bed and gazes in disbelief at her possessions. Only then does she notice her paperback book on the floor by the side of the bed, pages ripped out and scattered like leaves on a forest floor. She runs back downstairs and looks at the mess in the hall. It's her coat and rain jacket that have been thrown down; Adam's parka and Lilian's old gardening coat are still hanging where they were when she first arrived. She takes out her mobile with an unsteady hand and calls the police.

The person who takes the call tells her that a unit will be round to see her, and not to touch anything until the officers arrive. Nell makes sure the front door is secure and runs back up to her room. She stands by the bed and surveys the scene, wondering if she's missed anything. She gets down on her knees and peers under the bed. Nothing. She goes back downstairs and studies the front door, but there's no sign of any damage, and the windows at the back of the house are all intact. She calls Adam, but his phone goes to voicemail. She leaves him a message to ring her and tries Joyce, who answers after two rings.

'Hello.' She sounds breathless.

'It's Nell, Lilian's granddaughter.'

'Hello, Nell. Is everything all right?'

'Not really. The house has been broken into.' Nell's voice wobbles and she grips her mobile. She doesn't want to break down, not before the police come; she needs to maintain her composure. She's half listening out for the sound of a siren, but doubts it will be considered necessary, as she told the operator there was no sign of anyone still being at the property.

'Oh my goodness.'

'What time did you leave?'

'Around midday. Is there a lot of damage? What's been taken?' Joyce sounds distressed. 'Have you called the police?'

'Yes, they're on their way. There isn't any sign of forced entry and it's only my stuff that has been disturbed.' She details what she's found.

'You poor love, you must be so shocked. Shall I come over?'

'Please, I'd like that.'

Joyce arrives before the police. An hour has passed since Nell made the call. Her grandmother's antique vase is untouched in the hall, as is Nell's painting. She shows Joyce the damage, reminding her not to touch anything. Joyce checks Adam's room, as Nell didn't feel it was appropriate and wouldn't have known whether anything had been taken, and confirms it looks untouched.

'Usual untidy state,' Joyce says, and makes her a cup of tea, adds two cubes of sugar.

'Get that down you,' she says.

Her kindness makes Nell want to cry even more.

'Have you spoken to Adam?' Joyce asks, setting her own tea down on the table.

'I haven't seen him today. I left him a message.' Nell sips her tea, which tastes incredibly sweet.

'I think the cavalry has arrived,' Joyce says, and the sound of a car pulling up in the drive can be heard. Nell jumps up, tea abandoned, and goes to the front door.

Two police officers get out of the car, one male and one female. The tall female introduces herself as PC Rosanna Cartwright and her colleague as PC Dixon. PC Dixon takes notes in a small notebook while PC Cartwright looks around the house, checking the doors and windows. Nell gives her account of what she encountered before investigating the scene. She mentions the tobacco smell.

'Do either of you smoke?' PC Dixon asks.

'No,' Nell replies as Joyce shakes her head.

'And the other occupant you mentioned, a Mr…' He consults his notepad.

'Harris,' Joyce says. 'He's the main resident, I suppose you'd call it; he's a relative of the owner, Mrs Wetherby.' She fills the officer in on the situation. 'His room doesn't appear to have been disturbed.'

'When did you last see Mr Harris?' he asks.

'I haven't seen him since yesterday,' Nell says.

'Me neither,' adds Joyce.

'Do either of you know the address of his partner?'

Neither of them do, and the police prepare to leave, telling them that they will be in contact again once they have done some investigations, although PC Cartwright impresses upon them that burglaries do, unfortunately, often go unsolved.

'There is one other thing,' Nell says, and she tells them about the feeling she had when she arrived that someone had been through her rucksack. 'You know when you can't prove it but you just have a gut feeling? It was like that. I just thought I'd mention it.'

'You did right to,' PC Cartwright reassures her, but Nell notices that PC Dixon doesn't note it in his pad.

'If you do speak to Adam, could you ask him to get in touch, please,' says Nell.

'Of course.'

She waits until they've backed out of the drive before closing the front door and going back inside.

Joyce is washing up the mugs from earlier.

'You didn't tell me about your rucksack,' she says, peeling off her rubber gloves and hanging them over the tap. A drop of water splashes into the sink, followed by another.

Nell shrugs. 'I'd only just met you. And it could have been either of you, no offence.'

'None taken,' Joyce says. 'I'll be interested to know what Adam has to say about all this.' Her gaze flicks towards the window.

A shrill sound interrupts them, making Nell jump.

'That's mine,' Joyce says, rummaging around in her handbag and pulling out a mobile, raising her eyebrows as she reads the display.

'Hello, Adam,' she says.

CHAPTER FIFTEEN

1991

Sarah feels strong hands pulling at her and an excruciating pain in her side as she tries to turn and see where David is. But her head is cradled tightly in something rigid and a man in a uniform is telling her not to move, speaking in a gentle voice that makes her want to cry.

'Just tell me,' she says. 'David, my David, is he OK, let me see him.' But no matter how hard she tries to push herself up, her body has lost all its strength. The man concentrates on getting her onto a stretcher and into the ambulance, and his face is kind but his eyes are full of pain and she fears the worst.

A terrible keening noise fills the air and a different man is saying, 'Mrs Wetherby, try to stay calm,' and Sarah knows from the unearthly sounds that Lilian is making that something bad has happened to David and it's all her fault. If only she had let him go into the house… And so it begins, this sequence of 'if onlys' with which she will try in vain to rewrite the script of her life.

In the ambulance, she remembers the baby. She grabs the paramedic's wrist and whispers that she is pregnant but she doesn't want anyone to know yet, and he strokes her arm and tells her she is going to the best place, where she and her baby will be looked after, and he is going to give her something to ease her pain. Sarah closes her eyes and succumbs to sleep.

When she next comes round she is in a hospital bed, and it is there that brutal words are spoken to her in a gentle voice by a doctor with kind eyes. Her husband is dead but her baby lives and she has to be strong for its sake. He must be telling her this because he can see that she doesn't want to live without David. He has to inject her with drugs to calm her down, and she returns to oblivion, which is the only place she wants to be. He assures her that the fact that she is pregnant has not been shared with her mother-in-law.

Next time she opens her eyes, Lilian is standing in front of her, and she closes them again. Lilian shakes her arm and forces her to listen. She tells her it's all her fault that David has gone and she wishes she had never come into his life. If she hadn't insisted on going out for dinner, David would still be with them today. Sarah knows she is right. She wonders what terrible crime she must have committed in a past life to warrant losing both her parents and her husband in road accidents.

Lilian arrives the following morning as Sarah is sipping a cup of tea laden with sugar, struggling to get the hot liquid past the sadness in her throat.

'The estate agent called,' she tells her. 'I told him you won't be wanting the cottage now that David is unable to provide for you.' Her eyes flash with triumph when she says this, and Sarah feels real hatred for the first time in her life. She has tried so hard to like Lilian, for David's sake. 'I've made an appointment for you on Saturday; he's preparing some viewings for you.'

'I don't understand,' Sarah says.

Lilian gives a barely perceptible shake of her head to convey the contempt she has for her no longer welcome daughter-in-law.

'I owe you nothing,' she says. 'We both know how we feel about one another, and I don't want you living in my house any more. You can stay until you've sorted out accommodation. The estate agent is finding you a flat to rent. I've told him I'll cover the deposit. It's up to you to come up with the rent.'

Sarah grips the sides of the bed. This proves how little Lilian cares about her. She pulls herself upright and looks the other woman square in the eye.

'Are you sure that's what David would have wanted?'

'I've always known what's best for David. I chose him when he had no one and gave him a life.' She waves her hand at Sarah in a dismissive gesture, looking towards the window. 'A life you stole from him. You couldn't possibly understand.'

Sarah closes her eyes and doesn't open them until she's heard the door close behind Lilian. At least she won't have to live in that house for much longer. She rests her hands on her stomach, where her future is snuggled. She will inform the estate agent that from now on he should deal with her alone, and she will find a suitable property for her and the baby. She will move out of Willow House next month, before she starts showing. She intends to work for as long as she can into her pregnancy, and the savings she has will keep her going after that.

All she had in the world was David, and David is no more. It's hard to stop crying. The nurses are kind, but they can't take away the hole that is gaping inside her, the hole she hopes her baby will one day fill. The baby Lilian must never find out about.

CHAPTER SIXTEEN

2019

Adam returns an hour later. He is wearing paint-spattered jeans and looks sweaty, his hair slightly damp. Joyce briefs him on the break-in and then leaves.

Nell's whole body feels tense. The incident has made her feel violated, and Joyce's sinister remark about Adam is running through her mind. Is he trying to drive her out? She doesn't really know him, after all.

'I got your message,' he says, looking around. 'I was in the middle of a job. What's been damaged? I can't see anything out of order down here. Is it all upstairs?'

'Just the hall and my room. My coats were thrown on the floor – only mine, which is a bit strange.' Nell watches him closely but he doesn't appear to react. 'And in my bedroom, all my stuff has been thrown about. My book was ripped apart.'

'What about my room? Lilian's?'

'No, as I said, only mine.'

He frowns. 'So none of Lil's stuff has been touched? No valuables taken or anything broken?'

Nell shakes her head. 'Not as far as I can tell. Joyce says nothing has been taken.' The more she repeats the story, she more she is convinced the break-in was deliberately directed at her.

'Are you OK?'

'Shaken up, that's all.'

'Did they take anything of yours?'

'No, my laptop was in the bag I had with me; there wasn't anything to take, to be honest. It's all a bit odd.'

'What did the police say?'

'They've taken down the details and they'll be in touch. It's odd that I've been targeted when I barely know anyone here; there's only you and Gran, Joyce and Jenny.'

'Jenny?'

'She works at the library. I've been trying to find out more about the family history.'

'What for?' A suspicious look enters his eyes. 'Why are you dredging up all this stuff? Lilian's too old to deal with it. She warned me you were trouble.'

'Trouble? I've as much right to be here as you, if not more, and I'm going nowhere. So can we drop the hostilities?'

'Don't tell me what to do – it's my job to look after this place.'

'And I get that.' Nell bites her cheek to stop herself blurting out how finding out about her mother has disrupted everything. She's not ready to share this with this man who she barely knows, cousin or not. Lilian had no right to keep stuff from her and she owes her some answers, no matter how old she is. 'Of course I'll be sensitive, I appreciate she isn't well, but I'm scared of being too late.'

'If she snuffs it, you mean.'

Nell shakes her head in exasperation. 'Have some respect. Do you know anything about my mother?'

'No, why would I? Like I said, we didn't really know Lil until recently.'

Nell pictures Joyce's face as she warned her to be careful of Adam. If only they hadn't been interrupted by the phone call. Her throat is dry and she wonders if it's too early for a drink. She has a bottle of white wine chilling in the fridge since yesterday and she could do with a glass now. She crosses to the fridge and takes it out.

'Fancy a glass?' she says.

'No, ta. Can't stand the stuff. Besides, I've got to get back to work. Better not go to a job bevvied up or I'll lose my contract.' He pauses. 'But thanks. It's hard, all this. I'm not being difficult, just looking out for Lil.'

'I understand. The police will most probably be getting in touch with you. They asked me a few questions that I don't really know the answers to.'

'What kind of questions?'

'Your address, your partner.'

'Mandy? What's she got to do with anything?'

'Nothing, it's just routine.'

'OK. Catch you later.'

She's changed her mind about the drink and pours herself a glass of water instead. She's put off tidying her room for long enough. As she sorts through her things, she can't help shuddering at the thought of her underwear spread out on the bed. Could it be the work of a random intruder, a pervert who gets off on messing with women's clothes? It's not as if the house is full of items of immediate value to sell on: no computer equipment or state-of-the-art television. There are some valuable bits and pieces – a vase in the living room that Lilian was forever telling her was worth quite a bit, and a couple of paintings – but only someone who knows about antiques would appreciate those. No, Nell doesn't think that is what this break-in is about. The shard of anxiety lodged inside her chest is telling her otherwise. But if it isn't Adam who is trying to drive her away, then who on earth could it be, and what are they afraid of her finding out?

That evening after she's eaten, she makes herself a coffee and drinks it in front of the television. A drama is on but she isn't really watching it; she's thinking about her family and how much she wants to be able to speak to Lilian again. She calls Hannah instead.

'Hey, I just got back from the gym. How's it going?'

'That sounds so normal. Meanwhile I'm living with a long-lost cousin and the house was broken into this afternoon.'

'No! Are you OK?'

'I'm fine, physically, but mentally…'

'Tell me everything.'

The conversation with Hannah lifts Nell's spirits, as she knew it would. Before she goes to bed, she washes up her dishes, checks the back door is locked and has just turned out the kitchen light when she hears a crash. Startled, she pauses in the dark, unsure whether to put the light back on. The noise came from outside. Her heart is thumping. Could it be Adam? He went out earlier. But what would he be doing around the back of the house?

She stares out through the window, her eyes adjusting to the dark. The garden is partially lit by moonlight, but she can't see any signs of an intruder. After a few moments she decides it must have been a cat or a fox knocking something over. Her heart rate has gone back to normal, but before she gets into bed, she peers out through the curtains at her bedroom window, checking the garden once again. She stands there for a while, but everything is silent and still.

CHAPTER SEVENTEEN

Nell springs out of bed at seven o'clock the following morning. She's had enough of the thoughts churning in her head. She puts her wetsuit on under a thick sweatshirt and jeans, packs a towel and a bottle of water and sets off for the beach. When she first left for London, what she missed most was swimming in the sea. She's swum in lidos and the Hampstead ponds, but nothing has come close to that feeling of being at one with the ocean: the rhythm of the waves, the tang of salt on her lips and the vast horizon ahead.

The beach is deserted save for a man in the distance throwing sticks to a dog, and a seagull perched on a rock that watches her as she peels off her clothes and leaves them weighted down with her trainers. She clenches her jaw as she steps into the icy water, then drives under the surface to get over the initial shock and sets off with a steady front crawl. The water is calm this morning and it only takes a few minutes before she's in the zone, the physical activity preparing her for the day ahead and whatever it brings. Does she get her love of swimming from her mother? she wonders, increasing her pace, determined to find answers.

An hour later, skin tingling, mind sharp, she's in the kitchen with a mug of coffee. She makes a call to the solicitor. 'Good morning, Mr Grayling.'

'Ms Wetherby,' he says in his reassuring tone. 'I'm just reading through my notes to refresh my memory. How can I be of assistance?'

Nell talks him through the events of the last few days.

'I see,' he says. 'Let me summarise the situation as I understand it. You've returned to Seahurst to find your grandmother has moved out and a relative unknown to you is looking after – and indeed residing in – the family property, and you want to know what your rights are.'

Nell nods. 'That's exactly it. I think this Adam is legit; there's a woman who comes in to clean the house who has known Lilian for years, and she verified the connection for me.'

'And her full name is…?'

'Joyce… Actually, I don't know her surname. I can find out for you and let you know.'

'Excellent. So what exactly is it you want me to do?'

'Mainly I'd like to know whether Lilian has purchased her new property and what her plans are for Willow House. My relationship with her is so strained, I don't want to ask her outright about the house, not straight away.' Nell is facing the window, and a small bird hops onto the windowsill. She feels a surge of emotion at its fragility. 'Mr Grayling, I want you to understand exactly where I'm coming from. I'm not interested in the house for financial gain or anything like that; I'm simply trying to establish exactly what happened to my mother, and why Lilian lied to me. That's the most important thing to me at the moment and I won't rest until I know the truth. If Adam suggests I move out, I will lose access to my grandmother's documents, which I believe are still in the house.'

'I understand,' Mr Grayling says. 'I can confirm that your grandmother's will is stored here and that Mr Harris is not represented by this firm. He may well have representation elsewhere. Leave it with me, and I'll find out what you need to know. A few phone calls should do it.'

Nell finishes her coffee and goes up to her grandmother's bedroom. She mentioned Lilian's documents to the solicitor, but in reality she has no idea what has been left in the house. The door resists her weight. She jiggles the handle. It's locked. Somebody obviously doesn't want her in there. Adam? Has Lilian told him to lock it? Is that what he meant earlier when he said he it was his job to look after the house? Or could it be Joyce? Who has a key?

She checks the other bedrooms, to no avail. Lilian could have taken everything to her bungalow, and she's got no chance of searching that. Idly she opens the large linen cupboard in one of the spare bedrooms. The fresh smell of washing powder makes her think of spring as a child, washing hanging on the line as she played in the garden. Her bed could do with changing, and she takes out a pile of duvet covers as she searches for a sheet. The rustling of plastic takes her by surprise. Stashed behind a stack of sheets are two dark-green Harrods carrier bags, with their distinctive gold lettering. She gives a wry smile; only the best for Lilian. She lifts them out and glances inside. They look to be full of photograph albums and papers. She puts the linen back and carries the bags to her room.

There are three albums, black and white photos in the oldest one. She flicks through it, her fingers fumbling, so eager is she to see what is inside. But her heart sinks as she turns page after page of landscapes. This is her grandfather's album – he was a keen amateur photographer – and contains nothing of any interest. But the second is more promising, more personal. People appear amongst the scenes, and she sees Lilian and Gerald on holiday, standing in front of the Blackpool Tower. Her pulse races as she spots a small boy with a bucket and spade; this must be David, her father. She lingers over the picture, full of wonder at seeing him in this way. Gerald captured people seemingly unawares, and she wonders why his photographs were never on display. Maybe they were when he was alive.

Her emotions are churned up by what she's seen and she puts the albums aside to be studied later, turning her attention to the papers. Most of them are bills, letters from the bank, nothing of interest. Frustrated, she turns to a bulkier envelope. This contains a stash of loose photographs. She sighs. It's going to take her ages to go through these, and she needs to pay full attention to the task. She thinks back to the sense she had that somebody was in her room. What if they were looking for something of Lilian's? She thinks back to the break-in, the mouse. Is somebody trying to tell her to stop digging?

She looks around for the best possible hiding place. Maybe she could ask Jenny to look after the stuff for her, but no, she hardly knows her. For now she has to be content with her rucksack while she devises a better plan. To be extra sure, she puts the bag right at the back of the linen cupboard.

She doesn't know exactly what she's up against, but she's convinced the answer lies in the past. If it's Adam who wants her out, he could easily change the locks. And if it isn't Adam, what lengths will this person go to to get rid of her?

CHAPTER EIGHTEEN

1992

When Sarah wakes, her surroundings are different. She's no longer in the small flat she has come to know as home, where her bedroom looks out over the park and the smell of cut grass wafts in when she opens the window. As soon as the estate agent had opened the front door, she'd known it was perfect for her and her baby. The room was big enough for her bed and a cot and it was within walking distance of a parade of shops.

She moves to sit up, and pain grips her insides. In a flash, she remembers the gush of her waters breaking, the frantic, albeit reluctant, call to Lilian, the only person she knows close by with a car. She'll never forget the look on Lilian's face when they'd bumped into one another in town. Sarah had been frozen to the spot when she saw the familiar figure approaching, the huge swelling under her dress impossible to conceal. Lilian had opened her mouth like a fish, then clamped her lips together and seized Sarah by the arm, sitting her down on a nearby bench and firing questions at her. The memory fades into a blur as she pushes herself up in slow motion, taking in the white walls, the curtained bays, the medical equipment nearby. There are only three other patients in the room, and all three of them are asleep, their babies beside them. She looks around frantically for Nell, starting to panic when she doesn't see her. Her baby should be with her. Her heart pounds and she struggles to get out of bed. A nurse wheels a drug trolley in.

'Where am I? Where's my baby?'

The nurse comes to her bedside. She has a smiley face, but Sarah can't smile back. She looks at a chart that hangs at the end of the bed. 'Dr Palmer is looking after you; he's the top doctor here, so you're in good hands. I'm sure he'll be coming to see you shortly. I'll send him a message to let him know you're awake, and he'll be along as soon as he can.'

'But what about Nell?'

'Nell?'

'My baby. She's all I have.' Sarah's throat is overtaken by sobs and she's no longer able to speak; her breathing is harsh and quick and panic flutters inside her chest. The nurse presses a button and a serious young man appears. Sarah remembers him asking her lots of questions earlier today, or was it yesterday?

'Your baby is safe and in good hands,' he tells her. 'You're being treated for an infection, so your family will be looking after her until you are well enough to go home.'

Sarah sits up. 'My family?' Her hands scrunch the sheets up tightly around her.

'You developed an infection; you've been very ill. We had a duty of care to report to your next of kin. Your mother-in-law, Mrs Wetherby, is perfectly capable—'

'I don't want that woman looking after my baby.' She is barely able to speak.

'I understand the terrible loss you have both experienced, but Mrs Wetherby has experience of bringing up her own son. She'll be living in the nursery you have set up for Nell.'

'Nursery?' Sarah says, tears welling at the thought of her cramped bedsit, the cot she's erected between the wall and the bed.

'Yes' – the doctor frowns – 'the nursery. You'll be able to rest and join her feeling refreshed. Motherhood is a demanding job for any woman, let alone one who's gone through what you have. You can take advantage of the experienced staff here and let them know your concerns, and they'll be able to prepare you and give you strategies for coping with your new situation. I only envisage you being here a couple of weeks, a month maximum. The main thing you need to do is rest. The nurse is going to give you some medication to calm you and help you sleep, and we can have another chat when you're feeling better. Your baby will benefit from a rested mother, believe me.'

The doctor looks concerned and Sarah senses that he is telling her the truth, but no matter how much sleep she gets, nothing will bring David back. She takes two tablets with a glass of water and feels her limbs relax as she lets go of all responsibility. Getting well will make her the good mother she craves to be. It's only when her conscious mind is quiet that she feels as if she is with her husband.

Sarah doesn't seen Nell for three weeks. She aches for her baby but is unable to express her feelings, so deep is the depression that encompasses her. The drugs help her sleep, and after two weeks she begins to feel better, stronger. She wants to go home. Not home to Lilian and the gaping chasm that was David, but to her bedsit. She resolves to stand up to her mother-in-law. She saw how Lilian smothered her son, but Nell does not belong to Lilian; she belongs to David and Sarah.

On the day she is discharged from hospital, Lilian arrives to collect her without Nell, telling her they will pick the baby up from home. But on arrival at Willow House, Sarah is horrified to find out that Lilian has cancelled the bedsit contract and moved her possessions back to Willow House, setting up a wooden cot in her old room. She can't fault the arrangement in any way, except for the absence of David and their shared moments here, which torment her as soon as she sets foot inside. A mobile with baby lambs hangs over the cot, and there is a collection of soft toys and rattles on the cupboard beside it, which Lilian has filled with nappies and dummies and all the myriad things a small baby needs.

'How could you end my tenancy on the bedsit? I can't live here, I won't.' Sarah glares at Lilian, this immovable force. Nell starts wailing and Sarah bursts into tears. Lilian gives her something to calm her down, telling the situation is only temporary, until she is completely better.

That first night, Sarah is woken by Nell's cries and is instantly awake and rushing to her daughter. But as Nell grizzles and beats at her with her tiny fists, Lilian appears silently in the doorway, her ghostly nightdress wafting out, startling Sarah, who cries out, making the baby wail even louder. Lilian almost snatches the child from her, and she can only watch as Nell settles and Lilian takes her off to her own room, leaving Sarah, arms hanging listlessly at her sides, no longer of any use to her child.

She wonders if she is to experience such humiliation every night, but after that evening Lilian leaves her to the baby's cries, which happen frequently throughout the night. Sarah snatches a half-hour's sleep only to be woken again when the gut-wrenching cries resume, and she peers into the scrunched-up little face, red with anger or hunger or whatever is distressing her. Nothing she does seems to settle her, and she seethes inwardly whenever Lilian is able to respond to Nell's needs, seeming instinctively to know exactly what to do. But she doesn't tell Sarah where she is going wrong; she just watches her with a scathing expression or rolls her eyes or tuts. Her barbed comments and poisonous looks eat away at the already frail confidence that Sarah built up in the hospital, and part of her wishes she was back there, allowed to sleep and worry about nothing but her own health.

She admits to herself that her mood is low and she needs help. Things aren't helped by her failure to breastfeed her daughter. After countless attempts, each more painful than the last, and lessons at the hospital, followed up by visits from her health worker, she has to abandon the task. She hears the nurse talking to Lilian in low tones, but she doesn't need to hear the words; she knows that they're discussing her failure as a mother.

Lilian makes up the bottles with disdain, telling Sarah how many women are unable to breastfeed and saying it in a way that makes it clear she disapproves of such women. Sarah clutches Nell to her and showers her with love. Her mood is like a heavy weight that is bearing down on her chest every morning, and it gets harder and harder to haul herself out of bed and face the day. But Lilian insists she get up every morning at seven, no matter that Nell has been crying all night and she has barely slept. She demands she get dressed and come down to breakfast when Sarah can barely open her eyes to see what is on her plate. When David was still here, Sarah could laugh and joke about Lilian's rules, which are immovable as a brick wall. Now, with Joyce gone too, she has no ally.

Lilian tells her that while she was in hospital, she established the best routine for the child. Nell is a good baby, she tells Sarah. She doesn't cry through the night like some children and has taken to the bottle without a problem. Sarah is thankful that the nurses encouraged her to express her milk while she was in hospital. Lilian has supposedly been feeding it to Nell, but there are also tins of formula in the cupboard, and she wonders if Nell has been given her milk at all.

She knows she needs to be strong for her baby, who has big round eyes and a small pixie face and the cutest, most perfect fingers and toes. She clutches her mother's finger and stares at her with her cornflower-blue eyes, then opens her mouth and coos. Sarah's heart melts with love and sadness and she makes a decision to visit the doctor and explain how she is feeling. Underneath all these new emotions that assault her as a first-time mother is the sea of grief that courses through her, waves rising and falling relentlessly throughout the day and night, and she frequently breaks down and weeps like the tide crashing onto the shore.

Winter is receding, but Lilian tells Sarah it is still too cold to take the baby out. Sarah can argue all she likes about the benefits of sunlight and vitamin D; Lilian cuts her down and makes her arguments appear futile. Sarah tries to move her next appointment with the health visitor to a time when Lilian is unavailable, but Lilian watches her like a hawk and monitors her phone calls. She says she is doing what the doctors asked of her by keeping a watchful eye on her because of her fragile health; it is a requirement of her discharge, and surely Sarah doesn't want to go back to hospital. The threat simmers between them.

'We can't forget your deception with the estate agent, now can we?' says Lilian, and Sarah crumples inside at the memory of the little cottage that was almost theirs. At night sometimes, when Nell is quiet, she likes to imagine herself living there with her daughter, but she knows that this is one of those fairy tales that were never meant for her.

The health visitor, Dawn, is a solid woman with a dependable face, who coos over Nell and weighs her and asks if there are any problems. Sarah opens her mouth to tell her about the ravaging effect lack of sleep is having on her and her inability to make decisions for her child because her mother-in-law is so overbearing, but Lilian ensures that it is Sarah who makes the tea and so she is absent from the room while the women have a hushed conversation. She tries to hurry back but drops a mug and spills tea over her feet, and Dawn remarks how jittery she is and asks if she is taking her medication. Lilian assures her that she will take good care of her and that Sarah is obeying the rules.

Sarah wants to run after the woman when she leaves, almost calls to her when she hesitates at the gate and looks back with a question in her eyes. But Lilian takes her arm and pulls her away from the door, her nails digging into Sarah's wrist and twisting the skin until it burns. 'I know what you're trying to do,' she says, and Sarah wonders how much longer she can live like this, in the invisible web spun by her mother-in-law that covers her, sticky and evil.

One morning, Lilian eyes her suspiciously as she eats a boiled egg with a slice of toast, thickly buttered. She needs her strength for her daughter. But when she takes the pram out and begins to load it with everything she needs to take Nell out for a walk through the park to the doctor's surgery, Lilian appears and asks her what she thinks she is doing, taking the child out on such a damp day. Sarah bows her head and feigns acquiescence, but she is formulating a plan.

When Lilian takes Nell from her, Sarah runs upstairs and opens the wardrobe, taking out the shoebox in which she has hidden the means to her freedom. She'd withdrawn the money for the estate agent on the day of the accident, ready to hand over in down payment.

But the box is empty; her savings are gone.

CHAPTER NINETEEN
2019

Nell lies awake listening out for Adam. She doesn't know whether to expect him or not. It's gone midnight and she doubts he'll turn up now, but she can't completely trust him. Each time she turns over in bed, the wooden frame creaks and she imagines the wood splitting under her. Unable to settle, she finds herself wondering about the names she's uncovered from her library research, Charles and Mary, her maternal grandparents, who she never knew. She wonders how she can get to the stories behind the facts. It's all very well looking up documents, but what she wants is a gem, hidden away amongst the dry words; she wants the people to come alive and tell her their own stories. Tomorrow she'll go back to the library and search through the old newspapers; she'd run out of time on her last visit. In such a small community, she might have some luck.

She falls asleep imagining her other grandmother, picturing her as the complete opposite of the only relative she has even known. A kindly woman with twinkling eyes and rosy cheeks, a smile creasing her face. A story-book grandmother.

A crash wakes her in the early hours and she sits bolt upright in bed, alert. She listens, but all she can hear is her own breathing and the hammering of her heart at the thought of this huge empty house, the cavernous rooms, a stranger lurking in the shadows. Or is it a stranger? That makes her heart beat even faster. She creeps out of bed, glancing at Adam's room, which is lit up by the moonlight pouring in through the landing window. She goes up the few stairs for a closer look. The door is open, the bed smooth, the cover neat and just so in the manner of Joyce's handiwork. Another night away for him, then.

Downstairs, the rooms are partially lit by the moon. At night-time these rooms give off a sense of being off limits, that somehow she is doing wrong by stepping into them. They are all empty as she passes through with her tentative tread, the doors and windows secure, and not even a breeze disturbs the garden. She heads upstairs again, unnerved. Back in her own room, she checks the linen cupboard; her rucksack is undisturbed.

She wakes early, immediately alert, recalling the night before and trying to remember the precise nature of the crash, what exactly might have caused it. She concludes it wasn't a human noise, more like a brick falling, and was probably related to the weather. She suppresses the inconvenient thought that there was no wind last night when she looked outside.

This morning, rain is loud on the windows, the sky dark; no chance of a swim today. She doesn't linger over her breakfast, but eats toast and drinks tea then packs her bag to spend the morning in town, needing a break from the house.

Afterwards, she isn't able to pinpoint what exactly made her turn around and look back at the house, but something makes her glance over her shoulder as she opens her umbrella, swearing under her breath as the spokes get stuck; and the glance becomes a stare and a pain in her chest as she sees what has been done to the fence that runs along the side of the house. This, then, was the cause of the noise in the night, and she has to grip the wall to steady herself.

YOU ARE NOT WELCOME HERE

Bright-red paint, the letters bleeding drips like tears, and Nell looks around, rigid with fear, although she knows the culprit is long gone. Rain batters her umbrella and she shivers, not entirely from the cold. The damage can be painted over, but it's the meaning behind it she wonders about as she debates what to do. She'd rather catch the bus into the village, leave the fence and the problem behind her, but this needs to be reported. Just in case. In case she is right to be afraid.

She waits in the sitting room once she's made the phone call, watching out for the police car, which arrives twenty minutes later. She recognises the tall form of PC Rosanna Cartwright as she dips her head to unfold her long limbs from the car, and PC Dixon. This is an easy, non-threatening job for them; if only it felt the same for her.

PC Cartwright takes down details inside the house, while her colleague examines the fence and takes a photograph of the damage.

'Is this the first time you've noticed damage to the property?' she asks, and Nell goes over the details she's recounted before, the feeling of being uneasy when alone in the house. The scepticism in PC Cartwright's face is quickly masked with another question.

'Mr…' She consults her notes. '…Harris, the other resident, did he hear anything last night?'

'He didn't come home.'

She frowns. 'And is that usual behaviour for him?'

'I've not been here long enough to say. He's doing some work on the flat; when he's not here, he lives with his partner, Mandy. I don't know her surname.'

'OK.' PC Cartwright snaps her notebook shut. 'I'll be honest, there isn't much to go on, as there's no CCTV around here, but we'll do a door-to-door with the neighbours and see if anybody else heard any disturbance last night. We'll also speak to Mr Harris and ask him if he knows of any reason why he would be targeted.'

'I'm pretty sure this is directed at me,' Nell says. 'Ever since I've been back I've had the feeling that somebody wants me out of here.' She follows the policewoman out and locks the door behind her. 'I was just on my way out when I noticed the graffiti. I'll paint over it as soon as the rain stops.'

'Can we give you a lift into the village?' PC Cartwright asks. Spikes of rain are bouncing off the path, and the bus Nell was planning on getting will have long gone. Her shoes aren't waterproof and she doesn't have the energy to go back inside and change them.

'Yes please,' she says.

She doesn't feel safe until she is belted into the back of the police car, condensation fogging the windows so that she can no longer see the threatening red letters. But who wants her out so badly? Despite the warm air blowing out from the front of the car, she shivers.

CHAPTER TWENTY

The threat is still flashing in front of her eyes when Nell is dropped off in town. *You are not welcome here.* The sea lies in front of her and she stands looking out at it for a while, hair whipping around her face, recalling yesterday's swim. The waves that pulled her in, the spray in her face making her feel alive.

The route she walks is familiar. As she turns a corner and catches sight of her old primary school in the distance, her heart skips a beat and she stops short, allowing the long-forgotten sensations to swoop over her. She can see the path she used to take home, dragging her feet more and more the older she got, reluctant to leave the friendship and fun of school, wishing she had a mother and father to go home to, and then feeling consumed with guilt because she had her grandmother, and no matter that she was as prickly as the gorse bushes Nell is standing by, she had brought her up and was doing her best. *You ungrateful child.* Lilian's voice of old echoes in her head. She's no longer ungrateful, nor a child, and she's the closest relative her grandmother has. Lilian is old and sick and it's down to Nell to protect her, just as Lilian was protecting *her*; that was why she lied about her mother. But something still doesn't sit right.

She buys a coffee and sits in the small seating area at the back of the bakery. She enjoys a hit of coffee before placing a call to her boss.

'Hi, Stacey, it's Nell.'

'Hello. How's it going down there?'

Nell sighs. 'OK, I guess. My grandmother has got cancer – it's OK, she's having treatment, but I need to spend a bit more time with her and make sure she's coping. I definitely won't be back next week and I was wondering whether I could take more time off, another week maybe? We haven't got a date for my mother's funeral yet.' Hannah informed her there was a long wait at the funeral parlour, so it wouldn't be happening any time immediately.

While Stacey goes off to consult the work diary, Nell mulls over her dilemma. Because despite these moments of trauma, when past sensations and memories rise up to confront her and remind her of the childhood that she ran away from, another part of her is relishing the calming pace of the village, the beauty of the surrounding countryside, and she's questioning for the first time what she is doing in London. The alternative lurks at the edges of her mind. Could she really make a life for herself here? Make her peace with everything she's ever fought against?

Stacey comes back on the line. 'It's not a problem at all,' she says. 'It's a quiet period at the moment and you've got quite a bit of leave to take. Whatever you need, OK? You've so rarely asked for time off and your sickness record is exemplary. Take care of yourself, and I hope there's good news about your gran soon. Grandmothers are a bit special, aren't they?'

Her innocent remark leaves Nell with guilt stabbing at her soul. Her grandmother is special, but not in the way her boss means.

Inside the library, she's pleased to see Jenny's red ponytail bobbing in the distance. She's helping a woman with a baby to find a book.

'Let me know if you need anything else,' she says, before turning and spotting Nell. 'Oh hello.' She flashes a big smile at her. 'I was just thinking about you earlier. How are you?'

Nell smiles back, feeling instantly miles better. Jenny directs her to the newspaper section in the library. Actual papers are kept going back five years, with anything older being held on microfiche. Once she's shown Nell how to operate the slide viewer, she leaves her with the dates she's looking for.

Nell doesn't have a firm idea of what she wants exactly, or what precise dates she is searching for, so she types in the names Lilian and Gerald Wetherby. As she follows the links to her grandmother, she learns how she was an active participant in the life of the village, on this committee or that, organising cake sales and quiz evenings and for many years treasurer of the local branch of the Women's Institute. The Lilian portrayed in these snippets emerges as a lively person, sociable and engaged with all around her, a contrast to the stand-offish and distanced woman Nell grew up with. Gerald is mentioned less, usually only as an adjunct to his wife, accompanying her to various functions, the pair of them donating generous amounts to charity. Nell's mood dips as she realises the effect her father's death had on her grandmother, how Lilian withdrew from village life.

Peering at the screen gives her a headache and back cramp, and she stands up and walks about, willing energy into her body. She needs to toughen up against this lethargy that invades her when reading about the hardships her relatives have been through.

Next she does a search for her maternal grandparents, Charles and Mary Henderson. Like Lilian, Mary is linked to the Women's Institute, and also the church; at one point she even held office as mayor. She beams from a photograph, resplendent in her red finery, gold chains hanging around her neck. Once she is mayor, there are numerous references to her visiting schools, village fairs and charities. Charles is pictured on a couple of occasions, a portly man with a thick moustache, clearly thrilled with his wife's success. Nell imagines that Mary, like Lilian, is the strong woman driving this couple. She skims through the articles until she reaches a headline that grabs her attention.

FORMER TOWN MAYOR AND HUSBAND
KILLED IN SPANISH TRAGEDY

Former mayor of Seahurst Mary Henderson and her husband Charles were killed yesterday in a road accident in Torremolinos while holidaying in the Spanish town. The couple were driving a rental car and came to grief on one of the notorious bends in the road, the car veering off the road and over a cliff. Mary was mayor of Seahurst from 1971 to 1972 and devoted much of her time to charity work. The couple leave behind their daughter Sarah, aged seven.

Close friends of the Hendersons Gerald and Lilian Wetherby will be arranging a memorial service that will take place in the village on 17 September. A private family funeral will be held next week.

The article is dated 17 August 1973.

Nell sits back in shock at the words 'close friends'. She'd had no idea both her sets of grandparents knew each other. Why had Lilian never mentioned that? Her heart is also full of pain for her mother. Imagine losing your parents in that manner; no wonder she had a difficult life. And then to lose her husband in a similar fashion when they had their whole married life ahead of them. She sits with her head in her hands and allows the feelings of helplessness to consume her. Can she face looking up her parents' accident? Cold sweat slides down her back. A hand lands on her shoulder and she gasps out loud.

'I didn't mean to make you jump.' It's the librarian.

'It's OK.' Nell smiles awkwardly. 'I was miles away.'

'I just wanted to let you know we're closing for lunch in five minutes.'

'OK, thanks. I'll close this down.' If it hadn't been for the earlier incident she'd have had plenty of time. Reluctantly she closes down the microfiche, full of renewed anger with Lilian for hiding the truth from her, for not trying to make it work with Sarah. And how could she never even mention the fact that she was friends with Sarah's parents? More than ever she is determined to find out what happened to drive her mother away.

Back at the house, she retrieves her rucksack from the linen cupboard and sorts her grandmother's papers into piles on the large wooden kitchen table. The majority of them are bills, but despite her frustration, she keeps going, ignoring the ache in her back from hunching over the table, for if she finds the tiniest thing to do with her background, it will be worth it.

She almost misses it. A thick cream sheet of writing paper tucked inside a leaflet from the local council. She would never have found it if the leaflet hadn't slipped from her grasp and fallen to the floor, revealing the corner of the paper sticking out. She seizes it and studies the handwriting, the confident curls of the letters catching Nell unawares. It's been years since she saw her grandmother's handwriting, and the unexpected sight is curiously personal. She holds the sheet of paper to the light.

> I am gathering the facts, preparing my case, while I decide what action I need to take. You don't think I'll let you get away with it, do you?
>
> Lilian

She shakes the envelope out; clearly a page is missing. Frustrated, she studies the fragment again, willing herself to read between the lines, but there is so little to go on.

She goes back to the pile of bills and sorts through them once again, taking everything out of the envelopes, but no matter how many times she searches the pile, she has to resign herself to the fact that the rest of the letter is not there. If only she had the first page. She takes a photograph of the letter before stashing it in her room, between the sheet and the mattress on her bed.

The police call while she's having some soup, to report that they haven't found out anything about the break-in or the graffiti and there have been no other incidents in the neighbourhood. Nell wasn't expecting anything else. The call has unsettled her, though, and, not relishing the prospect of an evening alone in the house, she texts Jenny and asks her if she wants to go for a drink when she finishes work. They arrange to meet in the Fisherman's Arms at eight.

CHAPTER TWENTY-ONE
1992

Sarah finds Lilian in the sitting room. Without preamble, she demands to know where her money has gone. Lilian leads her to the kitchen, gets her to sit down and explain what she means. What money is she talking about?

'You're not alone,' she says. 'I've also lost precious items. That's why we no longer have a cleaner.' She doesn't accuse Joyce outright, but the implication hangs in the air with Lilian's sickly lavender perfume. Sarah stares at the table, unable to swallow down the nauseous feeling that is lodged in her throat. She liked Joyce.

Lilian makes her a cup of tea and takes Nell off to the park, to give Sarah some time to think, something she has far too much of. She remembers how urgent her morning routine used to be; how much life has changed; how she longed to have time to linger over breakfast instead of gobbling down mouthfuls as she packed her bag and rushed out of the house to catch the bus. Now she has that luxury, which is anything but as she longs for David and the bedsit she found and lost. Most days her time is filled up with Nell and her needs; everything takes twice as long as it should do, as Nell is a difficult baby and Sarah has so little energy. She doesn't blame Nell; she believes the child has internalised the loss of her father and is absorbing the frosty atmosphere between Lilian and herself. She tries to take Nell up to her room as much as possible, to make up for missing out on those early days of bonding when they were separated, but Lilian is always finding excuses to call her downstairs and to take over the baby whenever possible.

Sarah sits for a while and formulates a plan. She needs money, and fast. She washes her cup so that Lilian has nothing to chastise her for and calls the doctor's surgery.

'Sarah!' Maria, the practice manager, sounds pleased to hear from her. There's a moment of silence where Sarah knows she is weighing up whether to mention the accident, not wanting to upset her, but she goes for the safe option, the easy option, and Sarah is grateful, because she can't talk about David without tearing up.

'How are you? How's the little one? Nell, isn't it?'

'Yes, she's beautiful,' Sarah says. 'Hard work – she cries a lot – but that's to be expected.'

'You're so lucky to have family support,' Maria says.

Sarah grimaces. *My mother-in-law is taking over my life* is what she wants to say, but it will sound ungrateful and she doesn't know Maria well enough to reach out.

'Have you met any other young mothers? That was a huge help to me when my kids were tiny; we bonded at antenatal classes and the kids all grew up together, mostly amicably.' She laughs. 'Those women are my best friends today; their support was massive.'

'I didn't meet anybody,' Sarah says. She avoided the antenatal classes, too depressed to socialise with other people. 'But I might try and find a group now. How's everything going with you, and the surgery?'

'Oh, we're fine, Tim's got a promotion so we see even less of one another, but that suits me. And the surgery is the same as ever. Non-stop. We all miss you.'

'That's what I was ringing about,' Sarah says. 'I'm ready to come back to work now. I can't wait, actually. Just part-time, of course, whatever hours suit you.' Lilian will make a fuss whatever hours she decides, but Sarah is determined to stand up to her.

'Oh,' Maria says, and there's a moment of silence where Sarah feels uneasy. Maria clears her throat. Sarah grips the phone. 'I don't understand. I understood you weren't coming back.'

'What do you mean?'

'Your mother-in-law – such a lovely woman, she sounded so concerned about you – she rang and told us you were unwell.' Sarah grips the phone tighter. What has Lilian been saying about her? Her palms are sweating. 'She said you'd decided not to come back. How working with the public took it out of you. She told us how sorry you were, but what with the baby and everything else that has happened… I'm *so* sorry, by the way, that you've been having the most awful time. We wanted to come round and see you, but your mother-in-law said it wasn't a good time. So the thing is' – she clears her throat again – 'I've taken someone else on. I don't have any spare hours at the moment.'

Sarah sits down on the chair behind her with a bump. Lilian knows she planned to go back to work.

'But that's a mistake. She had no right to do that. Why didn't you check with me first before getting someone else in?'

Maria's voice is softer. 'I'm sorry, Sarah, I really am, but why would I question what I was being told? Lilian told me about the depression, and I do understand, it's so hard with a small child, let alone your circumstances. She also warned me you might want to come back when you weren't ready and she was only following the doctor's advice for you to rest. She's got your best interests at heart. We all have.'

Sarah slumps in the chair. She'd set her hopes on going back to work, had been looking forward to this phone call, and now her hopes have been shattered. Maria is a decisive woman and she knows there's no point asking her to change her mind. Sarah still has her pride, and she won't beg.

Maria suggests meeting for a coffee and Sarah says she'll be in touch, but she won't. Despite this all being Lilian's fault, she can't help blaming Maria for not checking with her first.

She yawns and her body aches for sleep, but the previous night's row is preying on her mind. It all started after dinner, when Lilian told her she was taking a bath, and that she'd have to keep an eye on Nell as she was extra grizzly.

'Of course, she's my baby,' Sarah said, relishing the chance to be alone with her daughter for once. She switched the television on for background noise and cuddled Nell to her, enjoying the warmth of her skin and the flutter of her tiny heart, like the wings of a moth in the night. Her eyes drooped and she watched Nell as she slept, the tiniest movement mesmerising her until she in turn fell asleep.

She woke to a loud cry. Lilian was kneeling beside her, so close that her sickly lavender aroma made Sarah cough, and she was shocked by how repulsed she felt.

'Nell is on the floor! Whatever do you think you're doing, falling asleep like that? I've only been upstairs for twenty minutes. I was as quick as I could be, because I knew something like this might happen.'

Sarah was confused; the television was switched off. In truth it was only a tiny drop from the sofa onto the thick carpet, but her heart thumped at the idea that she might have harmed her baby. She tried to take her from Lilian's arms.

'No you don't,' Lilian said. 'You'll only drop her again. Have you been taking your medication?'

'Of course,' Sarah said, wiping tears from her cheeks. How could she not? Lilian made sure she took it every day, standing over her until the glass of water was empty. Sarah didn't like the way the tablets made her feel; the one she took at night was supposed to relax her, but she daren't fall asleep lest Nell waken, and so she felt wired and frantic most of the time, her nerves running through her like an electric current.

A quick glance at the clock told her it was ten o'clock – the last thing she remembered was *Coronation Street* being on, so she must have been asleep for longer than Lilian had said; the medication was muddling her mind.

Later, when Nell was settled in her cot and Sarah was sitting up in bed, Lilian came in with her night-time tablet.

'It might be better if you thought about giving her up,' she said. 'It's clearly too much for you, given your state of mind.'

Sarah gripped hold of the side of the cot.

'How could you say such a thing?'

'I'm only saying what you know deep down is true. The accident earlier could have been so much worse; as it is, she was only slightly winded, but if I hadn't been here, well, I dread to think what might have happened.'

Sarah didn't quite see how it could have been worse, but her mind had become blurry and confused as the medicine entered her system. Perhaps Lilian was right.

'Sleep on it,' Lilian said, a smile on her face. Sarah knew the expression hid nasty thoughts.

She blinks hard and brings herself into the present. The job section in the paper only fills a single page, but she is prepared to do anything to get out of the house and back on the job ladder. Maria will write her a good reference, she is sure. She circles a cleaning job, her heart sinking a little, and wonders if she has the energy. Ignoring her doubts, she calls the number only to be told the position has been filled. The only other jobs on the page are for cab drivers, and the mere thought of driving makes her break out in a sweat.

Lilian and Nell aren't back yet and the morning stretches in front of her like a chasm. The clock ticks into the room and she goes upstairs to get away from the irritating noise. She draws the curtains and lies down on her bed fully clothed.

She wants to go to sleep and never wake up. Maybe Lilian is right and Nell would be better off without her.

Dear Mary,

No doubt I'm the last person you expected to hear from. I imagine you'll be reading this feverishly, heart knocking slightly: *could she possibly know?*

Well yes, I do, I know everything about your sordid secret.

Writing this down feels therapeutic already. I've never been one of those women who confides in all and sundry, twittering with a female friend over cups of tea and confidences served up with a slice of lemon cake, secrets spilling over a glass of wine or two.

Up until last week I suppose I'd have said you were my best friend, although the term makes me shudder somewhat – it's the sort of thing adolescents say, not grown women. I'm glad I've kept my business private, because now that I know how you have betrayed me, it would make me shudder to think you'd heard my innermost feelings expressed. Our friendship worked because you accepted my limitations, my desire for privacy; I could just *be* with you. Unlike others, you didn't judge me for being a difficult woman. Everyone does things for a reason. My reason for writing this is to make you suffer.

Anyway, I digress, Mary. You'll be wondering how I found out – is your skin itching and hot at the thoughts this letter is conjuring up in you? *Has she been watching me? What has she seen?* Oh yes, I've been watching you, Mary, you and him, for a while now.

Obviously Gerald has no idea. Not yet. But he will, oh yes, he will. I've got it all planned out. My world changed last week. May the fifth it was, a sunny day, which makes it worse somehow. Sun on an upturned face makes the spirits rise, and I had no reason to feel anything but hopeful, anticipating the summer ahead, always my favourite season. I'd been for a walk by the sea after lunch, as I do most days. Gerald was at work and I anticipated an afternoon in the garden, some gentle weeding before reading my book on the bench under the apple tree.

As I turned into our street, I saw you, Mary, so distinctive in your pale-yellow spring coat, scurrying down our front path. You never walk fast, so that aroused my suspicions – if you had been calling for me, what would have made you hurry away? The moment I saw Gerald's car parked further along the street, my heart began to thud and it was my turn to hurry, wanting to know what awaited me. It was hard to get my key into the lock as my hand had started shaking, and when I pushed through the door, Gerald emerged at the top of the stairs, straightening his tie, broad smile on his face, story prepared. I asked him what he was doing home, and he launched into an explanation of forgetting a document he needed. He kissed me on the cheek as he left the house, leaving a hint of spicy aftershave in my nostrils. It made me sneeze. Foolish man had no idea his shirt was untucked at the back.

To an untrained eye, the bedroom looked undisturbed, the pillows plumped just so, the cover smooth and unwrinkled. Too smooth. It was my book that gave it away, lying face down, only the blurb on the back page visible. A Margaret Yorke it was. A murderer in a small village. She writes so credibly about domestic matters. I like things to be just so and my book is always neatly squared parallel to my pillow, face up. Fussy, Gerald calls it. Stupid of him, to not notice this detail. You, Mary, no doubt, snooping into my things, not content with just my husband. What else have you looked at in my bedside table? Have you held my string of pearls up against your naked neck, imagined yourself in my diamond earrings? The thought made my blood slide like ice through my veins. Joyce would have noticed. Joyce knows exactly how I like my things to be. That's why she's been with us for so long.

In one short burst of time the two people closest to me had dealt me a terrible blow. Despite knowing the conclusion I'd jumped to was right, I needed further evidence.

I am gathering the facts, preparing my case, while I decide what action I need to take. You don't think I'll let you get away with it, do you?

Lilian

CHAPTER TWENTY-TWO
2019

The pub has a cosy feel to it, with low ceilings, three different rooms and tables tucked in nooks and crannies. It's reasonably full, but not crowded. As Nell is there first, she texts Jenny to see what she likes to drink.

Red wine, Jenny texts back.

She chooses a table with two comfy chairs by a fire and orders a bottle of red wine. Jenny appears in the doorway, stamping her feet against the cold, her red hair wrapped in a multicoloured scarf.

'Good choice of seat,' she says. 'It's freezing this evening.' She holds her hands out to the fire. 'What do you think of my favourite pub?'

'It's great,' Nell says.

'Good job, as it's the only one in the village.'

'I'm just glad to be out of the house, to be honest.' She tells Jenny about the graffiti, which she has now painted over with some black paint she found in the shed.

'And you think this was directed at you? Some locals are a bit funny about Londoners coming in and buying up all the best property and then it sitting empty for most of the year. It might just be that they think you're not from around here. On the other hand, if they do know who you are, they might think you're planning to take over the house.'

'I guess. It certainly feels personal. And I can't help thinking Adam is behind it. He's not comfortable with me being in the house, I can tell. But I'm going nowhere.'

'Good,' Jenny says.

'I've got more time off work, arranged it this morning. Despite everything that's been happening, this place feels like a respite from London. My life there is so hectic, my job's full-on, and most evenings I can't switch off from my work emails. That's what comes of being a perfectionist, I guess.'

'You organise events, don't you? How did you get into that?'

'By chance, actually. I was sharing a flat with a woman who worked in marketing, and she loved it, so I signed up to a temp agency. I had the experience of working in the florist's—'

'You worked in a florist's? How lovely. I've always thought people who do that must be happy people, surrounded by beautiful flowers and colours all day.'

'Yes, I had a Saturday job at Alison's Petals; it used to be on the square, but it's closed down now. I wonder what happened to Alison. She was lovely to me. I still feel bad about leaving her in the lurch like I did.' She drinks some wine. 'I did a marketing course eventually and worked my way up to the events job. But I loved my job at the florist's and part of me has always wanted to do something more creative again.'

'You could open up your own florist's,' Jenny says, her eyes shining. 'My dream is to run a bookshop with a café.'

'That sounds great,' Nell says. 'Here's to our dreams.'

They clink glasses and laugh.

'I imagine your job isn't quite as stressful as mine,' she says.

'You try dealing with the general public.' Jenny grins. 'But no, you're right, it's pretty low-key most of the time.'

She spends the next half-hour regaling Nell with tales of entertaining customers, and Nell feels her shoulders lose the tension that has been gripping her since the incident this morning. She hasn't heard from Adam; every now and then she glances at her phone, half expecting him to text her about the graffiti.

The fire crackles, warming her legs, and she feels safe here, unlike the way she's been feeling in the house, with its floors full of empty rooms. Around them the sounds of conversation flitter in and out of earshot, a woman's laugh, a man's deep chuckle. She relaxes and rolls her sleeves up as the warmth of the fire reaches the left-hand side of her body, and for the first time in ages she forgets about the mark on her arm.

Her attention is drawn by a commotion at the bar, as a man protests he's been given the wrong change. It's the first sign of discord in a public place she's seen since she arrived here, and for an instant she's reminded of London, where people are more brash, impatient, quick to argue. She sees Jenny looking at her arm and then glancing away, and she rolls her sleeve down, embarrassed.

'I hate it. I usually cover it up. Up until recently I believed it was a birthmark.'

Jenny shakes her head. 'It doesn't look like a birthmark to me,' Jenny says. 'It looks more like a burn scar.' Nell freezes. 'Oh no, what have I said?'

Nell stares into the fire. 'You're right, but I've only just found out. Lilian spoke to me about my mother when I went to see her. She told me it was her fault I got burnt.' She holds her arm out so that the firelight illuminates her skin.

'May I?' Jenny runs her finger over the top of the scar, her finger cool as it touches the hard skin. 'See the way it feels thicker; that's not how a birthmark feels.'

'Australia, I've always called it,' Nell says, and Jenny smiles.

'It does look like that, doesn't it? I think you should own it, be proud of who you are.' She lowers her voice, then whispers theatrically, 'I don't tell many people this, but I've got a birthmark on my right buttock, so I should know.' She taps her nose and they both laugh. 'Did Lilian tell you much about your mother?'

Nell's eyes fill with tears, and she blinks hard.

'It's OK,' Jenny says. 'I can see you're not ready.' She tops their glasses up. 'But you know you can talk to me.'

'I found out more today,' Nell says. 'I can't believe she lied to me for all those years.' She tells Jenny about the newspaper article, and the letter she discovered.

'That sounds really sinister. You've no idea who it was to?'

Nell shakes her head. 'I'm scared it was to my mother.'

'Oh no, surely not.'

'I just don't know what to believe any more. This whole secrecy thing is so weird – losing a close friend in a car crash is a big thing; why hide it from me?'

'Perhaps it was too painful? Some people blank things out, whole memories even, as a coping mechanism.'

'Maybe, but it doesn't make sense to me. This close friend was my grandmother. There has to be a bigger reason for not wanting me to know about it. I won't rest until I know.'

'Don't look so down in the dumps. I've got some news for you that will cheer you up. I've spoken to my gran, and she remembers your grandparents, Mary and…'

'Charles. Oh, that's wonderful. Especially with what I know about the car crash. Would she want to talk to me?'

'Would my grandmother want to talk?' Jenny laughs. 'Only someone who hasn't met her would ask that question. Delving into her past memories is her favourite thing.'

'Can I come and see her?'

'That might be a bit difficult – she lives in Canada.'

'Oh.'

'No worries, though. I've asked her to write down exactly what she remembers about them, and she'll be only too happy to help. She's like that, my gran, she's lovely.' Her eyes are shining along with the glow of the fire.

'Jenny.' They both look up to see a man wearing a striped woolly jumper. His shock of white hair takes on an orange hue from the firelight. He's holding two pints of lager, the amber liquid a similar shade to his hair.

'Hi, Gary,' she says. 'This is Nell. She's staying at Willow House.'

'You must know Adam Harris, then.'

'Yes, he's doing the place up. How do you know him?'

'He did a job for me last year, redecorated my house. I ran into him last week, in here as a matter of fact. Looks like he's fallen on his feet this time, jammy bugger.'

Nell and Jenny exchange a quizzical look.

'What do you mean?' Jenny asks.

'You must know Willow House?' She nods. 'Well apparently his mum stands to inherit it. It must be worth a bomb. No wonder he's doing it up. I bet he can't wait to put it on the market.'

'He's actually converting the space so that Mrs Wetherby can move back in,' Nell says. 'She is still alive, you know.'

Gary's face changes at her indignant tone. 'Hey, I'm just the messenger. That's what he told me. Who are you—'

'Hey, Gary, we're dying of thirst over here. Stop chatting up the ladies.' A group of men sitting at a nearby table are looking over at them, laughing.

'I'd better go before I get lynched. Remember me to your mother, Jenny.'

Nell's cheeks are warm both from Gary's remarks and the fire. 'Well that was interesting,' she says. 'Adam hasn't said anything about his mother inheriting to me.'

'He wouldn't, would he?'

'I've asked Lilian's solicitor to clarify the house situation. I must chase him.'

'Wouldn't it be you that inherits? Or did she cut you off completely?'

'No, she didn't, at least not as far as I know. But it would explain why Adam hasn't exactly been welcoming. He suggested Lilian didn't want me living there, but she told me it was OK. Something doesn't feel right.'

'I hope all this isn't going to drive you back to London.' Jenny's cheeks colour up. 'I like having you here.'

'Don't worry, I'm not going anywhere until I get some answers,' Nell says. 'And thanks. Which reminds me, I must call Hannah, my best friend in London. She'll be wondering what's happened to me.' Her phone buzzes with a text. 'Be funny if that was her now, wouldn't it?' She opens the message. 'Oh, it's the landlord from my mother's flat.' She quickly scans the words. 'He wants me to make the final visit there tomorrow – gosh, that's soon. But I'll do it. That way I can call in on the neighbour. She's one of the few people who knew my mother recently.'

CHAPTER TWENTY-THREE

Nell alights from the train at Victoria and is thrust into a bustle of activity as commuters in smart suits march past her, darting and tutting through groups of tourists hauling cases and clutching maps. She joins a queue at a coffee stand and absorbs the thrum of activity and noise around her. As she sits and stirs her coffee, she is glad she doesn't have to step into this throng at speed and dash to her office, to be faced with a burgeoning inbox and a pile of expectations. She adds an extra sugar to her coffee to counter the bitter taste in her mouth at the thought of what she is about to do. Her mobile rings as she's sitting there. It's Tom, her mother's neighbour. She left him a message last night, alerting him to her visit and expressing her wish to meet his wife.

'Thanks for getting back to me,' she says. 'I'm on my way to the flat now.'

'And Moira's looking forward to meeting you. What time will you be here?'

Nell looks at her watch. Her coffee is finished and she can't put this off any longer.

'Should be about forty minutes.'

'Why don't you call in once you've done what you need to do? We're not going anywhere. No doubt you'll welcome some company after you've been to the flat. It can't be easy for you.'

Nell wells up at his words, but manages to thank him without her voice cracking. A woman is speaking in the background.

'Oh yes,' Tom says. 'Moira has something she needs to give you.'

Nell gets to her feet and puts her cup in her bag, eager to know what they have for her. She pushes through the cluster of people in front of the departure board, necks craned awaiting information, and heads off down the escalator towards the Tube. Through the loudspeaker system, passengers are being informed that the train for Seahurst at platform 11 is ready to depart, and Nell is surprised to find she wishes she was back there instead of plunging underground with so many others.

Visiting her mother's flat feels different this time. On the first visit she was filled with incomprehension and felt as though she was in a daze. This time she is armed with more facts, and has a certain level of resignation at the knowledge of her mother's existence. She walks towards the block trying to imagine her mother's thoughts as she took this same route. Did she think about Nell, the baby she'd abandoned? Was she really this uncaring character her grandmother painted? How would Nell ever find out the truth?

Outside the tower block, she looks up, trying to pick out her mother's flat, but it's impossible. She settles on one in the corner with an empty balcony, a pigeon perched on the edge surveying the estate. Did her mother like living here? With kind neighbours prepared to look out for her, why did she choose to remain so isolated?

When she lets herself in to the flat, she can't escape the fusty odour, and once inside she feels the sense of desolation. She checks every inch of each room, but she hasn't missed anything, and when she leaves, she's confident the landlord will be satisfied. She makes sure the balcony door is secure, but doesn't venture out, not wanting to see the city through her mother's lonely eyes. She hopes whoever moves in will be happier here, will be loved.

A woman answers the door at the neighbouring flat, the smell of baking drifting out from behind her. She's small and round like Mrs Pepperpot.

'You must be Nell,' she says. 'Come on in. Tom has told me all about you coming before; I was gutted to have missed you.' Her blue eyes flit over Nell's face and she catches Nell watching her. 'Sorry for staring, love. I can't help it. You're very like her, you know.'

'Moira,' her husband calls, and she ushers Nell inside, where the heating is on and the kitchen smells of coffee. 'You never knew her, did you?'

'No,' Nell says.

'Have you done everything you came to do?'

She nods. 'The landlord asked me to check the flat over; he wants to rent it out next week.'

'As soon as that?' Moira says. 'It's terribly sad. If it helps, I'd like to tell you the little I know about your mother. I don't suppose many people have been able to bring her alive for you. She was a funny little thing. If I hadn't made the effort in the first place, I doubt we'd ever have spoken. It's not right, I used to say to my husband, for someone to be so solitary. She never had any visitors you know, well, not until later…'

'Let the girl sit down, Moira, for goodness' sake,' Tom says, pulling out a chair for Nell. 'She'll be wanting a cup of tea, or coffee, won't you, love?'

'Yes please, tea would be great,' Nell says, sitting down at the kitchen table, her legs heavy. She finds tea more comforting than coffee. Tom makes a pot as Moira puts some scones on a plate and pushes a butter dish and knife towards Nell. But Nell's stomach is tensed up at what she is going to hear, and she shakes her head. 'No thanks. I'm a little nervous.'

'Oh you poor thing. Tom tells me you're from London yourself?'

'I live here, yes, but I grew up in Seahurst – that's where my… where Sarah was from originally. I'm staying there at the moment while I sort things out. This has all been a terrible shock because I didn't even know she was here. So if there's anything you can tell me about her, what she was like…'

'Frustrating is the word that comes to mind,' Moira says, sitting down opposite Nell. 'I could see she was having a hard time of it – she worked really long hours and she never went out as far as we could tell – but she was incredibly proud. I asked her so many times if she needed anything, invited her over, but she always declined. It was as if she was hiding something she didn't want us to find out, or maybe she was just one of those people who are so shy they don't want to mix with anyone. She wouldn't tell me if anything was wrong, even though she knew she could.

'She had the most terrible cough and it used to worry me. I could hear her hacking through the walls, and I went round one day, made her some hot lemon and honey, just like my mother used to, and she was so grateful it brought tears to my eyes. She promised she'd go to the doctor, said she'd been trying to get an appointment but it was never suitable for her work. She said she'd lose her job if she took time off, but that can't be right, can it? It's these zero-hours contracts, you see, terrible thing they are. You don't turn, up you don't get paid and there's always some other mug waiting to be exploited. I'm devastated at what happened and I've been chastising myself ever since that I didn't force help on her, but you can't, can you? Hindsight is all very well, but at least I was able to do one thing for her, which is why I'm so pleased to see you.'

'Oh?' Nell asks.

'She asked me to keep something for her. It was quite bizarre, but maybe you'll be able to shed some light on it. It was after the visitor came.'

'Visitor?'

'Yes. Recently, it was, not long before she passed away. It was unusual, because she was the only person who ever came to see her as far as we could recall. Excluding the postman, of course, or tradespeople. An elderly woman, she was – Tom got in the lift with her, that's how we knew. In her seventies, thick grey hair, very severely cut. Sarah called round here the next day and asked me to look after something for her. Once she'd passed on, I didn't know what to do with it.'

'What is it?' Nell grips the seat of her chair, unsure what she's hoping for.

'A book. I'll just pop to my bedroom and get it.'

Moira pushes her chair back and Nell listens to the clock ticking, counting the beats until she returns. The woman Moira described could be Lilian, although her hair isn't severely cut, but is she up to travelling? Nell plays with the locket around her neck. To have another souvenir of her mother would be wonderful and might contain more clues for her to follow.

Moira comes back in and puts a notebook bound with an elastic strap in front of her. 'I had a quick look inside; it's some kind of diary. She asked me to keep it safe but didn't give me any kind of explanation, poor love. She'd never asked anything of me before, and of course I said yes.' She blinks hard, and Tom reaches across and pats her arm.

'Don't upset yourself, love.' He looks at Nell. 'She blames herself, you see, although there's nothing she could have done. Sarah was ill, love, it was out of your hands.'

'I should have pressed her, but you don't, do you? She said she didn't want anybody to find the book if they broke into her flat. It seemed an odd thing to say. These flats are pretty secure.' She shakes her head in frustration. 'I can't stop thinking about it. I hope you can forgive me.'

Nell picks up the book, which has a black cardboard cover. She peeks inside, sees words cramped together, her mother's handwriting. It's a gift as precious as the necklace.

'I don't understand why you would blame yourself,' she says, frowning.

'Because Sarah was frightened, love,' Tom says. 'When we asked her about the woman who came round, she had a look of sheer terror in her eyes.'

CHAPTER TWENTY-FOUR

1992

Lilian is out at her Women's Institute meeting. Sarah looks forward to these nights spent alone with Nell. She needs to prove to Lilian she's a capable mother. Her favourite times are when Nell slumbers in her arms; she hopes that her daughter is feeling the transmission of motherly love through her skin, in a way that she should have been feeling with breastfeeding. But Nell is crawling now, getting into things, and she is restless and squirms on Sarah's lap. Sarah puts some toys on the floor and lies down next to her baby, who is contained by some large cushions, which she loves to push against and bounce off, chuckling. She clutches a bright green rattle and waves it in the air, mouth open in a gummy smile. Sarah smiles back at her, almost able to laugh. These moments are special, as she feels herself healing. She hangs on to them when she slides back into her negative thoughts. Her money might be gone, but she'll find another way to escape.

She picks Nell up when she goes into the kitchen to fetch herself a cup of peppermint tea. She thinks of evenings spent with David when his mother was out: spritzers for her and a bottle or two of beer for him, peanuts in bowls and fooling around on the sofa like a couple of teenagers. He felt Lilian's restrictions too, although he would never say a word against her; Sarah clenches her fists when she thinks about it.

Lilian is due back fairly soon and she can only imagine what she would have to say if she were to catch her drinking wine. Tea is safer with the medication she's taking; it's been months since she drank any alcohol, and she was never a big drinker anyway. She clutches the cup to her chest to keep it out of Nell's reach, settles her back against the cushions and watches her daughter play with her favourite doll, pushing it against the cushion as if she wants it to sit up like Mummy. Sarah can't wait for her daughter to start calling her Mummy. At present she's making lots of noises, but none of them sounds like words. Lilian repeats 'Granny' to her often, which Sarah hopes is far too hard for a child to say.

Sarah is smiling as she watches Nell, feeling warm and comfortable for the first time in ages, and she doesn't notice her thoughts swimming and her eyes drooping. Three noises wake her simultaneously: the front door slamming, Lilian shouting and Nell crying as if someone has stamped on her.

But it's so much worse.

Nell is screaming, and Lilian is rushing into the kitchen with the baby in her arms. Nell's legs are kicking and her face is the colour of a tomato. Sarah takes in the scene through bleary eyes: the mug on the floor, a pool of liquid seeping into the carpet, steam rising. She feels it and it is very hot. She must have fallen asleep and dropped her tea. Panic rises in her. She rushes into the kitchen, where Lilian is holding Nell's arm under the cold tap while the baby yells as if she is being tortured.

'How could you?' Lilian's face is white with rage. 'Look at her arm, look what you've done.'

Sarah moves closer to her baby and stares in horror at the angry red welt on Nell's arm, vivid against her white skin. She reaches out to hold her, but Lilian hisses at her.

'Keep away from her. Haven't you done enough damage?' She turns her back so she's a barrier between Sarah and her daughter. 'There, there,' she says. 'I'm taking you to the hospital, you poor little thing.'

Sarah's mouth is open and she clutches her arms around herself in anguish at what she's done. If Lilian is taking Nell to hospital, the burn must be very bad.

'Let me hold her,' she says, desperate to be close to her baby, to comfort her. How can she ever make it up to her? She prays it isn't as bad as it looks, that it will just be a surface burn. A cup of tea can't do that much damage, surely?

'No,' Lilian says. 'Get the car keys.'

'But…' Sarah itches to hold her baby in her arms.

'Hurry up.'

Lilian ignores her for the ten minutes it takes Sarah to drive to the hospital, her eyes meeting her mother-in-law's in the driver's mirror, the hostility in Lilian's glare making her hands shake.

'It's my baby, she's burnt – help her, please,' she says to the receptionist in A&E. Tears are pouring down her face.

Lilian and Nell are ushered into a cubicle by an efficient-looking nurse, Sarah trailing behind like a spare part. Another nurse taps her on the shoulder. 'It's OK, your baby is in safe hands.' Sarah's pulse is still racing, and she shoves her hand over her mouth. The nurse does her best to reassure her. 'She's going to be fine, I promise.'

'I did this, I'm a terrible mother.' Sarah can't help the words spilling out. 'I fell asleep, I've been so tired, I must have spilled my tea.' She still can't believe how it happened so quickly. She can only have dropped off for seconds. And where did Lilian come from? It felt as if she'd only just gone out.

'You aren't a terrible mother,' says the nurse. 'Accidents happen.'

Nell is calmer once the doctor has seen to her. Her tiny arm is covered in a temporary dressing and she's been given some medication to help with the pain and calm her down.

'Please don't blame yourself,' the nurse says. 'Worst-case scenario, she may have a scar, but there won't be any other lasting damage.' *It could have been so much worse.* Sarah finishes the sentence in her head.

When Sarah goes out into the corridor with Nell, Lilian stays behind with the nurse. As she tries to listen in to their hushed conversation, she recognises the stab of feeling she feels when she thinks about Lilian: it is fear.

She doesn't want the kind nurse to leave, but she does. Later, when the woman from social services arrives, with her earnest look and her battered briefcase, Sarah knows this is Lilian's doing. Marion, the social worker, asks lots of questions and writes copious notes and says she will have to report the incident to her superior. Sarah tries to explain how she's got it wrong, how she adores her child and perhaps there's a problem with her medication.

'Is it right to feel so tired, so low, so incapable? This isn't me.'

Marion exchanges meaningful looks with Lilian and scribbles more lines in her notebook, fast, as if she has so much to say. Sarah wishes Marion could have seen her at work, laughing with patients and zipping through her tasks, her buoyant mood when she showed off her wedding ring. She wants to take her baby and run from the hospital.

Dear Mary,

The evidence I needed was presented to me the following week. Do you know how humiliating it was to hear gossip about your affair with my husband? I was at the village summer fete, browsing jars of jam made by Annie Williams, chatting idly about the correct amount of sugar to use – oh how I wish I could go back to that innocent time – when Gladys Sandwell appeared, attracted by the plump strawberries in Annie's jam, or so I thought, until she tapped my arm and asked in a low tone if she could have a word. I assumed she was going to offer to take over the post of treasurer at the WI, as she's been trying to do for months; surely she wasn't going to bribe me with a pot of strawberry jam?

In that precise moment, the church bell pealed out three harsh chimes, drowning out Gladys's words and forcing her to repeat her treacherous revelations: she'd seen Gerald entwined with you, Mary, in the church grounds, partially hidden by a large gravestone. Obviously she had to tell me: a married man should never break his marriage vows. She crossed herself at that and said she'd been praying for the three of us. A damning phrase indeed; no longer were Gerald and I to be *the two of us*, one of so many seemingly small changes, like the shard that lodges in my chest ever since that moment, the shard that drives me to act.

Naturally Gladys was unaware of my acute distress. My face remained inscrutable and I held my head high as I dismissed her cruel insinuations. I crossed the lush green lawn at my usual pace and didn't slump until I was in the ladies' in the church and closing the cubicle door behind me. But seconds later the horror continued as, sitting on the closed toilet with my head in my hands, I heard Celia's unmistakable nasal voice, at a lower pitch than usual, telling Annie Williams, 'The secret's out. Gladys has told her.' My whole body stiffened. The entire village would soon know, and I was to be a laughing stock.

Do you know how hard it is to hold my head up high in this town where secrets cannot exist? To stand in the queue at the bakery and see Annie's pitying look as she pops an extra bread roll into my regular order and we both pretend not to have noticed. You know how proud I am, Mary, and all this is your doing. My only comfort is that you know me so well, and you know I won't let it lie. I will punish you. You'll be as distraught as I am, Mary, when I've finished with you.

Lilian

CHAPTER TWENTY-FIVE
2019

Nell stashes her bag in the overhead rack and places the notebook on the table. It's three minutes until departure. A family enter the carriage but head past her; whistles are blowing and the train doors close with a satisfying clunk. She has the table to herself. She's promised to contact Tom and Moira when she has details of the funeral, and is happy she'll be seeing them again. They feel like a piece of her mother.

She opens the notebook as if it's a fragile document. Sarah's handwriting is in black biro and her letters are large and curly like a teenager's, easy to read. Each entry is headed with a date. The book starts in 1998. Nell was six that year. By then she would have understood that she had no mother. She used to pretend to her classmates that her grandmother was her childminder, that her mother was away. She didn't want to stand out by being different, even at the age of six.

'Tea, coffee, sandwiches.' A train guard pushes a trolley into the carriage, dragging her thoughts away from her mother, and she has to refocus and remind herself where she is. She buys a bottle of water to help ease the dryness of her throat, brought on by the fear at what she might find in the notebook. When the trolley has moved on, clattering through the carriage, she turns to the last few pages. What she longs to know is what happened to her mother in the last few weeks of her life, her curiosity piqued by Moira's observations.

> I couldn't write in here last night because my head was so bad. It's happened every day this week and it makes it hard to do my job. Everything takes an age to do and Mr Dean called me into his office last night because I hadn't finished my floor. Cynthia came down to see where I was – we all usually meet up to go down to reception and sign out – and she helped me as best she could. She told me I should go to the doctor if it happens again but I convinced her it was a one-off. She knows we can't take time off sick, because look what happened to Maisie when she did; her contract was ended that day. I can't afford to lose this job.

She leans back and closes her eyes to hold in her emotions. Her mother feels like a living, breathing part of her now and she's unused to how emotional it makes her feel. She has always had an emptiness inside her, and her mother is filling that space. She drinks some water and turns to the beginning of the notebook. It is immediately apparent that this is not Sarah's only diary, as the first entry begins mid sentence. She squeezes her eyes shut in frustration.

She forces herself to read through her mother's experiences of struggling to exist in an unfriendly city, her attention piqued when she sees her grandmother's name for the first time, the word heavy on the page as if Sarah pressed extra hard with her pen as she spelled out the name.

> During the day I try to shut the memories out, but when I go to sleep at night they flood in front of my eyes and I replay the scene of my failure over and over. I'd had it

planned for so long, and that morning I'd tried and failed not to be excited – if my plan worked, I'd be travelling back with my daughter. I can't believe so many years have passed since then; so many failed attempts to get her back.

Lilian opened the door to me, her eyes narrowing when she recognised me. She peered over my shoulder as if she was expecting me to have a burly minder in tow. Seeing her in the flesh, I nearly lost my nerve. She was taller than I remember, with that haughty expression as she looked down at me from the doorstep.

I told her I wanted to speak to her about Nell, and she mentioned the agreement straight away, but I insisted she let me in. Her lavender perfume assaulted me as she led me through the dark hall and I tried not to gag. The kitchen was unchanged, the once new farmhouse kitchen now dated and as tired as I felt.

I launched straight into what I wanted to say; I'd memorised it like a wedding speech. I told her I was sick when I signed the agreement and she couldn't expect me to stick to it forever. She must have known I was going to come back for Nell as soon as I was better. I told her about my job, and that I was well mentally and ready to look after my daughter. Since I'd stopped the medication, my head had cleared.

The whole time I was there, I was looking around for signs of Nell – toys, clothes, the sound of her voice – desperate to see my little girl, but I should have known better. Lilian didn't keep photos or drawings or anything frivolous, or leave things lying around. She was like a spider controlling her web. When I could hold on no longer, I asked to see her.

She laughed at me, said it was out of the question and that the document we'd signed was legally binding. Nell was settled and doing well at boarding school and I would only be a disruption. A disruption! I am her mother. And boarding school? Lilian has shipped her away like she did with me. I was even more determined to get her back in that moment, and my emotions got the better of me. I pleaded with her to tell me where she was, but she kept her lips tight, her face in that reprimanding expression she always wore in my presence.

I left – there was no point staying – and told her she'd be hearing from my solicitor. But the scorn in her eyes told me she knew I was bluffing. Since then I've been looking at boarding schools nearby, trying to work out which one Nell is at. But what good would it do even if I did track her down? A dark cloud of depression is back, weakening my spirit and making it harder for me to believe I will ever see my daughter again.

Nell only realises the train has arrived at Seahurst when the cleaner appears and she looks around to see she's the last person left in the carriage. Sarah's words are heavy stones pressing down on her chest. She didn't go to boarding school. Was Sarah's memory wrong, or was Lilian lying? And if so, why? More questions for her to put to her grandmother.

As soon as she gets back to the house, she retrieves the albums and the envelope of photos from the linen cupboard. Downstairs, she lays them all out on the table. The loose ones are a mixture of sizes, and some have writing on the back. Those without people in are of no interest, and she sets them aside. Next she makes a pile of any with Lilian in, and the rest go in a second pile. Then she makes herself a cup of tea and starts on the albums, marking certain pages with slips of paper. What she's looking for are photos with Mary and Charles in. She's intrigued by the changes in Lilian over the years, surprised at her vanity and how she liked to pose for Gerald, always well turned out in her expensive outfits and carefully coiffed hair.

After an hour, she's left with a handful of photos documenting a long friendship. She spreads them out on the table in front of her. Three are of particular interest to her. The first is of two young mothers standing in a park, both with pushchairs in front of them. Lilian's dark hair is arranged in a magnificent bouffant style; Mary has her long blonde hair parted in the middle. Both are wearing belted raincoats and look chic. Nell's attention is drawn to the children, her parents as toddlers, both chubby and laughing, looking at one another.

The next photo she has picked out is of her two sets of grandparents standing together by a gate, arms slung around one another, all smiling, Gerald's attention caught by something off camera. Nell strokes her finger over Gerald's face. He looks kind and she wishes she'd known him. He looks like he would have been able to stand up to Lilian. But it's her mother, Sarah, she's riveted by. She looks to be about five, crouched down grinning, mud on her clothes. No sign of David in this one. Nell wonders what it was that made Lilian so loath to mention the other couple to her. Was there a falling-out in this group of friends? When did they stop being so happy and at ease in each other's company?

She turns to the last photo she's selected. The four of them again, on holiday. This time the background is a street lined with palm trees and the women are wearing dresses and sandals, the men shorts. Somewhere hot, abroad, but there's no other clue to the location. Mary is holding an ice cream and Gerald has his camera on a strap around his neck: the stereotypical tourist. Their expressions are serious this time, as if the photographer forgot to remind them to smile. She puts the two photographs together and compares the expressions of the adults. Something about them bugs her, but she can't think what it is. Was this the holiday on which Mary and Charles were killed?

She's about to go back to the albums when her mobile rings. It's Jenny.

'Hi,' she says. 'How was London?'

'Very interesting. The neighbour had my mother's diary.'

'Wow, that's dynamite. Have you read it yet?'

'I've started, but it's hard going.'

'I bet. I've got news for you too. I've had an email from Gran. She's written down what she remembers about your grandparents. Give me your email address and I'll send it over.'

A swoop of excitement rushes through Nell.

'That's fabulous. Thanks so much, Jenny.'

'Cool. Let's speak tomorrow. I'm going on a date tonight. Wish me luck.'

'You won't need it,' Nell says. 'Can you send the email before you go?'

'I'm doing it now.'

She is aware of her heart pumping. She doesn't have to wait long.

Dear Jenny,

Thank you for sending me on this trip down memory lane. I'm lucky, aren't I, that my memory is good. Unlike your mother, who forgets everything I say to her! I've enjoyed writing it all down. I've always said I should write a book.

I knew Mary and Charles because we all went to Seahurst primary school. Charles was a couple of years older so I didn't really know him, but Mary was in my class. We weren't friends as such and I only have a vague memory of her, and we went on to different secondary schools. As adults we always said hello, but that was the extent of the relationship really. Mostly I read about her and Lilian in the local paper; both of them were pretty active in the community, Lilian organised the village show. The cake-baking competition was hotly contested, I remember. I even entered one year and somehow managed to come third!

You said you wanted to know everything, which is why I'm telling you this next part, although I fear it may upset you. I first heard talk of it at the village fete, and I'll admit I thought it was nonsense and dismissed it as idle gossip – you know what Seahurst is like!

What I heard was that Mary Henderson was having an affair with Gerald Wetherby, and I'm afraid it was true, because I saw the evidence with my own eyes. I was out for dinner with Harry, your grandad, and he'd driven us out to the country to a little restaurant he knew. It was a fair way from Seahurst, so I was astonished when I saw Gerald seated at a table when we arrived. He looked flustered, and it was only when his companion appeared from the ladies' that I realised it was Mary he was with, and not Lilian. No doubt they'd chosen the place as it was so far from town. I pretended not to notice, and they left soon after.

It wasn't long after that that they all went on holiday together, which took me by surprise though really it was none of my business. But no matter what had gone on, all was forgotten when Charles and Mary died. It was big news locally, as you can imagine. Lilian organised a huge funeral, black horse drawing the hearse through the village and everyone coming out to pay their respects. For what it's worth, I didn't tell a soul what I knew.

You also asked about Lilian's son David. I didn't know him at all – obviously I read about the accident, everybody did – but I do recall her daughter-in-law, Sarah. It was so tragic for her, poor love. None of us knew what to say to her. I used to say hello to her in the village, but there was only one occasion when we had any real interaction. She was trying to manoeuvre the pram into the post office – you'll know how narrow the entrance is. I offered to wait with the baby while she went outside – that will be your friend Nell; how strange that you've met up with her all these years later – and she was so grateful. Such a cute little baby she was, all wrapped up in a lemon-coloured jumper and clutching a toy sheep. We had a little chat when Sarah came out, and I could see how much she was grieving. She doted on that baby. I could see her looking over her shoulder at us the whole time she was in the post office to make sure she was OK, even though I wasn't a complete stranger.

The phone clatters from Nell's hand, and her vision blurs with tears.

She doted on that baby.

So what happened to make her mother leave her?

CHAPTER TWENTY-SIX

The house phone rings, startling Nell out of her thoughts, and she rushes into the hall.

'Hello,' she says.

She hears someone breathing.

'Hello, can you hear me?'

The breathing gets louder, but whoever it is says nothing. Puzzled, she puts the phone down. It rings again. She snatches it up, determined to give the caller a mouthful, but the voice at the end of the line throws her. It's Lilian.

'How are you?' Nell asks.

'I'm as well as can be expected. I'd like to see you again. Could you come tomorrow afternoon?'

'Yes. Just one thing before I go. Do you know that your bedroom is locked?'

'Yes.' Lilian's reply is short and clipped and Nell can imagine her drumming her fingers impatiently, the large diamond in her engagement ring flashing where it catches the light. 'There is no reason for anybody to go into my bedroom. I asked Adam to lock it.'

'He must have forgotten then, because it was open when I first got here.'

'And how do you know that? Why do you want to go into my room?'

'I don't. I…' She lets the sentence trail off, not wanting to tell Lilian about the break-in.

'I'll see you at three o'clock tomorrow.'

Nell goes upstairs and tries the door to Lilian's room again. Now that it's forbidden, she wants to get in there more than ever. What is it her grandmother doesn't want her to see? She hears the front door opening and goes to the top of the stairs to see Joyce letting herself in.

'Hello, Nell.' Joyce hangs her coat up in the hallway.

'Hi. How are you?'

'Mustn't grumble. I wasn't sure you'd still be here, what with the break-in, and Adam told me about the writing on the fence. I can see where it's been painted over. Vandals. Have you heard anything from the police?'

'Only that they haven't caught anyone. Apart from you, Lilian and Adam, does anyone else hold keys to this place?'

'Not that I know of.'

'Do you clean Lilian's bedroom?'

'No, it's locked. She doesn't want anyone going in there while she's not here.'

'It wasn't locked when I first arrived.'

'Wasn't it? Must have been a mistake.'

'That's what she told me, but isn't it a bit weird? You won't be able to clean, and it's not as if she's only away for a week.'

'I'm not paid to wonder if things are weird. This is Lilian's house and I do as I'm instructed. Have you decided how long you're staying?'

'Oh, for a while yet. Apart from talking more to Lilian, I'd forgotten how nice it is to be back by the sea. The city is so polluted; when I'm at home, I wake up each day feeling chesty. That hasn't happened here once.'

'I don't have time to be going down to the beach.' Joyce puts on her overall and her rubber gloves. 'I'm cleaning downstairs now.'

'I'll get out of your way. I think I'll go for a walk.'

Nell goes upstairs and fetches the envelope of photos from the linen cupboard. She takes an apple and a bottle of water from the kitchen and walks down to the beach. She tucks her hair under her woolly hat and pulls her scarf tighter around her neck. The bright-yellow scarf was a Christmas present from Stacey, and she loves it. She misses Stacey but not work. She walks along the front for ten minutes before reaching a sheltered spot under the sand dunes. She finds a comfortable nook to sit in and eats her apple, watching the rough waves fighting one another to get to the shore. The cold air makes her skin tingle, and the waves mesmerise her. It was here she made the decision to leave all those years ago, as she watched a seagull lift itself up from the water's edge and soar into the sky.

She angles her body so the photos are protected from the wind and sorts through them until she finds the photo she was looking for: four friends standing by a gate, her mother in the foreground, Mary's hair flying up in the wind, a laugh on her face. Had they been on a picnic? Had they eaten hard-boiled eggs and drunk from flasks of tea? What had they talked about? As the only child, Sarah would have been the centre of their attention; children always lighten a mood. She searches the picture for clues although she has no idea what she's looking for. She'll show it to Lilian, ask her about it. These were her close friends, and Mary was having an affair with her husband, so it was understandable that she never mentioned them. Nell has yet to encounter the death of a loved one; perhaps grief would lead her the same way, to shut herself off as Lilian did, closing the drawbridge to her castle. She even got rid of Joyce. She'll ask her about that too.

A sprinkle of spray on the page makes her jump. The tide has crept closer while she's been engrossed in her thoughts. Ten minutes more and her feet will be wet.

The wind is against her on the walk back, hair flying despite her hat, and she thinks of Mary again.

CHAPTER TWENTY-SEVEN

1992

Sarah can't get the doctor's words out of her head. *Scarred for life.* Nell has an angry red blemish the shape of Australia on her lower arm. As her arm grows, so will the scar, and the doctor says that because the burn went deep into the layers of skin, it will be permanent. He puts a positive spin on it – it's not on her face, it can be covered, it's no more unsightly than a birthmark – tries to get Sarah to smile, but she knows her baby is marked now, the blemish a permanent reminder of what an incompetent mother she is.

She acquiesces when Lilian insists she move the cot into her bedroom, because she can't trust Sarah to be alone with Nell, although Sarah thinks this is wrong. She is Nell's mother after all, and with a bit of guidance she will learn to cope with these everyday challenges. This is what the textbook tells her, filled with knowledge she has devoured, but the book has disappeared from her room. Lilian denies having ever seen it, and so Sarah concludes that too must have been removed by Joyce; she was right not to trust her with her confidences.

Lilian tells her she will take over Nell's routine so she'll be able to catch up on her sleep and get herself back into condition to take care of her baby. Sarah lies awake listening to Nell crying in the room next door, unable to go to her child. She cries along with her, tears flooding the pillow she presses her face into, and lets out a silent scream. Her eyes are rimmed with dark circles, her hair hangs lank because she doesn't have the energy to wash it, and there doesn't seem to be any point in getting up in the morning. Lilian hovers around her like an omnipresent wasp that she doesn't have the strength to bat away. How can Sarah stand up to her when she has nowhere else to go? The easiest thing for her to do is sleep. She doesn't even need to go to the doctor's any more, because Lilian handles her medication.

The social worker, Marion, calls round to the house the week after Nell was taken to the hospital. She interviews Sarah alone, although Lilian bangs pots around in the kitchen, making her presence heard. Marion has a catalogue of incidents Lilian has reported to her where Sarah was negligent with her child. She is round and energetic and speaks to Sarah as if she is a five-year-old, her face serious as she warns her that if it wasn't for Lilian, she would most likely have had her child taken away from her already. Sarah tries to tell her of her low mood and her desperate grief for her husband, but Marion pats her knee and tells her she is on the right medication and she should be feeling better soon, especially with the new temporary sleeping arrangement. She chides Sarah for not appreciating and making the most of the help she is getting from her wonderful mother-in-law.

The next time Marion visits, Lilian tells her how she bathes and feeds her granddaughter while Sarah tries to protest that Lilian doesn't give her a chance to do it herself. Marion tells her Lilian knows what she is doing and what Sarah is capable of. Sarah's mind is fuzzy a lot of the time now, as if a ball of cotton wool is lodged between her ears, and she can't think of the right words to say, so mostly she stays silent. Marion shakes her head as she leaves, after an earnest conversation with Lilian on the doorstep that Sarah can't hear.

Sarah lies in bed and thinks about her medication. She's been taking it for so long, two tablets in the morning and two tablets at night, yet it doesn't seem to be helping; if anything, it is making her feel worse. She resolves not to take it any more. The following morning, when Lilian arrives with her tea and two white tablets, Sarah tells her of her revelation, excited that she may have hit on what is making her feel so bad.

But Lilian is aghast at this idea. She sits down on the edge of the bed, takes Sarah's hand in a rare moment of warmth that brings tears to her eyes and tells her that it is the medication that is keeping her alive. She knows how Sarah feels, she tells her, the desire to give up on life and be with David; she herself felt like that at first but they have to keep going for the child. She keeps control of the pills, she says, because she fears Sarah might overdose.

Sarah breaks down and cries at the realisation that Lilian knows her secret desire to escape from this world. She has let her daughter down in the worst possible way. She doesn't even like to admit to herself that she no longer has a deep yearning to see Nell, to hold her and rock her close and make her promises she is incapable of keeping; how can she, who can barely get herself up or string a sentence together, possibly sort out a home for her child away from this woman who controls them like puppets? Every move she makes is thwarted.

'Children absorb our moods,' Lilian says, 'and Nell is picking up this sadness. That's why I've been keeping her away from you. It's for the best of reasons, you must understand.' And Sarah wants to believe her, to see a softening of Lilian's features, but Lilian's eyes dart about and won't fix on hers.

'Think about it,' she says. 'I can help you sort yourself out. Hospital isn't the answer; I think you just need a break from here.'

Sarah thinks of the sea and how much she loves living here, but when did she last go to the beach for a swim? She knows that Lilian is right: being with Nell in her current state isn't helping her. She can't go for walks because too many memories of happy times with David are to be found along the way: an embrace on this bench, a kiss behind that tree, eating ice creams, hair blowing in the wind, paddling at the water's edge hand in hand.

'Maybe you should get away from here for a while; I can look after Nell while you recover…' Lilian leaves the suggestion dangling like a rope. Sarah doesn't know whether to grab it like a lifeline or to hang herself with it.

For the next few days, Sarah thinks of nothing else; round and round like a merry-go-round go her thoughts, spinning faster as she considers whether she really could leave her baby, slowing down when she imagines how she'd feel about herself if she did. Under Lilian's care Nell is still waking at night, but she's sleeping more and is less whiny during the day. 'All she needs is a solid regime,' Lilian says. 'Stick to the routine and she'll learn to behave.' Sarah wishes her mother-in-law was kinder to Nell, gentler, how she would be if she had the strength, but she knows now she can never be a proper mother feeling the way she does. At last she reaches a decision.

'You're right,' she tells Lilian. 'I'm not well enough to look after Nell. I can't cope. She's better with you.'

Lilian nods. 'I'm glad you've seen sense.'

Sarah doesn't feel sensible, with her cloudy head and her inability to cope with daily life. Her insides are screaming that she's making the wrong decision for her baby, but her brain tells her otherwise. It's impossible for her to see any other way forward.

Lilian moves into efficient mode, drawing herself up tall.

'It's best you get far away from here, otherwise you'll want to come back and see her. The main concern is that the child be settled.' Sarah flinches at the words and a flicker of concern raises its head, but her own head is heavy and she has no energy to deal with it. 'You don't need to worry about money. In fact, I have a proposal for you. I've found a flat in London you can rent. I think the city is the best place for you. You'll have access to good hospitals and there will be more opportunities for work.' Sarah can't imagine ever working again. 'I'll take care of the rent for as long as you need, if you're willing to go along with my terms.'

Money is a constant worry to Sarah. Her marriage to David was so new, they hadn't got round to life insurance, to sorting out all the practical and financial arrangements that married couples make. Now she feels relief that at least for a while she won't have to think about that side of things. In the murk of her mind she believes deep down that once she's well, she'll be back to take Nell away with her and will be able to make up for lost time.

'I've drawn up a document that outlines my expectations. Take some time to read it, and then once it's signed we can organise the move. I'll make some tea and you can look through it now.'

Lilian appears to be in a hurry. Sarah's eyes are heavy. She doesn't want tea – everything tastes bitter lately; all she wants to do is sleep. While Lilian clinks cups in the kitchen, she stares at the document, rubbing her eyes and reading the first paragraph once, then going back to it because her mind can't unscramble the meaning behind the words. Three times she reads the sentences: 'I, Sarah Wetherby, hereby relinquish full control of my child to her paternal grandmother Lilian Wetherby in return for accommodation for life, namely monthly rent including deposit to the landlord. Lilian Wetherby will take full financial and parental responsibility for the child, ensuring she receives a good education and upbringing. There will be no visitation rights as I understand this will be detrimental to the child's welfare.'

There is more, but she can't take it in. She doesn't see it as a binding document. Lilian has drummed it into her for long enough that all she has to do is get better and she will be able to care for Nell again. She doesn't really want to leave her home town – the lure of the sea is still strong, and she is not familiar with London – but when Lilian comes in with the tea tray, she allays her fears, telling her the flat is in a good area and close to one of the best hospitals in the country.

Lilian smiles when she sees that Sarah has signed the document, which makes her feel nervous; she is even more surprised when Lilian eats a slice of the sponge cake she has brought in on a plate. To anyone who knows Lilian, who opposes eating between meals, it would appear she is celebrating.

Sarah excuses herself from the room; she is tired and can only think about laying her head on her soft goose-feather pillow and going back to sleep. Her sleep will be dreamless. London will be like a rehabilitation – she will get well and then come back for her daughter.

Sarah stands outside the Tube station and looks around her. People criss-cross in front of her and a sense of urgency and purpose fills the air. She has the keys to her flat and clutches a piece of paper with the address on it. Lilian told her to cross the main road outside the station and go left by the burger bar, where she will find the street where she is to live. She can't believe her mother-in-law has left her to find her own way like this; she was supposed to be driving her up to London to help her settle in, but she was called away to an emergency right at the last minute, and instead dropped Sarah off at the train station, shooting off in the car as soon as she had climbed out.

Sarah waits at the crossing outside the station. She notices litter on the street and how thick the air is around the busy traffic that crawls along in front of her. Smells of onions and meat drift out of the burger bar as she surveys the street in which she will live. She feels like she is outside herself, watching this woman do unexpected things. As she takes in her surroundings, she understands Lilian's plan: she will strive to get better quickly in order to escape from this area. The flat she is heading for is in a high-rise block, a grim slab of concrete, and she wants to rush back to Seahurst and inhale the smell of the sea.

Inside, the flat is bigger than she expected, but her heart is heavy as she walks through the rooms, thinking of the place she has left behind, wondering how her life has ended up at this point. The kitchen is small but has everything in it she needs, as Lilian promised; she even has her own washing machine. She opens the tall fridge and looks at the empty shelves for a long time, the responsibility of filling them with food, of looking after herself, pressing down on her. She leaves her bag on the bed and walks back through the flat, unlocking the balcony door with a key she finds on a hook. She is enormously grateful for this small square of outside space, which she has all to herself.

Two streets away she finds a small supermarket and buys herself some milk and bread and a box of tea bags. As an afterthought she adds butter and jam. This takes a while, as she stares at the shelves for ages, finding it almost impossible to make up her mind. A woman leans around her and tuts with disapproval, but Sarah barely notices her. People express their feelings more here, she notes, rather than gossiping and whispering behind curtains.

On the way back to the flat, in response to a stab of hunger, she stops at the burger bar and orders a greasy burger and fries, but only manages a few mouthfuls, pushing the plate away and instead sipping her tea. She spends an hour staring vacantly at the door, watching people hurry by: bent old men and youngsters with hair coloured pink, pierced eyebrows and biker boots. She feels anonymous here in her bland clothes and is glad that no one is paying attention to her. She doesn't belong.

When she gets back to the flat, in no hurry to arrive, her feet leaden, it is dark already and she realises that she has made a big mistake. She calls Lilian from the phone that hangs on the wall in her flat. It's a payphone and she feeds coins into it, which clang into the metal container, a jarring sound. But the number she learned by heart after her first date with David, when already he made her heart flutter and she knew she wanted to spend the rest of her life with him, results in a flat tone and the operator telling her that it is no longer available. She redials, cursing her clumsiness, although by now she is used to her inability to perform normal tasks. The message is repeated, as it is every time she redials, until she sinks uncomprehending to the floor and wonders how long it will be before she sees her daughter again.

CHAPTER TWENTY-EIGHT
2019

Something is missing. It takes Nell a moment to realise what is different about the hall. She stands in the centre, and moves slowly in a circle like a compass, studying the cabinet with ornaments inside, the bookshelves, the mirror on the wall. The painting! It's gone. Now she realises how obvious it is. The bare wall, the smudged rectangle where the canvas had hung for years. She loved that painting. Is that why it's disappeared?

She makes a coffee. Somebody is targeting her and she isn't sure why. The painting was special to her, a sixteenth-birthday present from Alison at the florist's. A beautiful white rose. Alison knew how she loved those roses and she'd asked her artist husband to paint it especially for her. It was the one item Nell regretted leaving behind, but she'd known it was safe in her grandmother's house, and Lilian hadn't minded it hanging there. By the time she was in more settled accommodation in London, relations with Lilian were so tense that she'd not wanted to come back to the house, with the arguments that would have entailed.

She stirs milk into the mug of coffee and sits at the kitchen table, mentally listing possibilities. Joyce moved the painting so that she can wash the wall; Adam took it down in preparation for redecorating. She adds a lump of sugar, a small cube of comfort. Other reasons for its disappearance are too ominous to think about.

She hears Adam's van pulling up outside. He comes in via the back door carrying a cardboard box.

'Phew,' he says, dropping it on the floor by the door. 'That weighs a ton.'

'What is it?' she asks.

'Metal brackets for the shelves I'm putting up.'

'Are you going to be redecorating the hall?'

'Yes, but not for ages yet. At the moment I'm concentrating on the conversion.'

'So you haven't moved the painting that was hanging there?'

'No.' He frowns. 'To be honest, I don't remember seeing a painting. Lilian's stuff isn't to my taste.'

Nell raises her mug. 'Do you want a tea or coffee? I've just made one.'

'No, you're all right. I need to get on with my work. Heave ho,' he says, lifting the box up and taking it through to the living room where the shelves are to be installed. He comes back through the kitchen, pausing at the back door before going outside.

'But thanks.' He pushes the door shut behind him with his foot.

It must have been Joyce. Nell dumps her mug in the sink and opens the fridge to see what she can cook this evening. She's hungry already. Aside from half a block of cheese and a sorry-looking courgette, there's nothing to work with. Stodge is what she fancies. So much for all the home cooking she was going to be doing while she no longer had work as an excuse. On the fridge door she spots a pizza leaflet. Adam must have stuck it there, as she can't imagine Lilian has ever ordered a pizza in her life. Her stomach growls at the thought, and she recalls with a jolt the last time she contemplated ordering pizza, but didn't get round to doing it because of the solicitor's letter. Back when all this started, which feels like a lifetime ago. Pizza tonight, and then she'll go shopping, get some fresh vegetables and start looking after herself.

On an impulse she goes into the garden and follows the sound of drilling to the far end of the garden. Adam is wearing protective glasses as he works on a piece of wood.

'Adam,' she shouts, waving to get his attention. 'Adam.' He stops drilling and looks up.

'Do you fancy a takeaway pizza? My treat. I'm ordering one for myself anyway.'

He hesitates, looking surprised, then nods.

'Yeah, great idea, cheers. Pepperoni for me, thick crust.'

'OK. I'll order it for seven p.m.' She smiles to herself as she walks back across the lawn.

Nell hears Adam taking a shower while she's on the phone to Hannah, updating her on the latest developments.

'So you're getting on all right with him?'

'I'll tell you after this evening. The pizza is a bit of a break-through. But we are cousins, so I want to make an effort.'

'Be careful. You don't know who's behind that graffiti.'

The doorbell cuts into their conversation.

'That'll be the pizza. Speak soon.'

She calls Adam on her way downstairs and he appears a few minutes later in a grey sweatshirt and a clean pair of jeans instead of his usual paint-spattered old clothes. He smells of lemons and his fringe flops down over his eyes.

'Good idea this,' he says, opening the fridge. 'Fancy a beer?'

'Great.'

He opens two bottles and hands one to her. The glass is frosty and the beer lovely and cold.

'What have you got?' he asks.

'Margarita with lots of mushrooms.'

He pulls a face. 'Me and vegetables don't get on so well. It's pepperoni every time for me.'

'Pizza is a once-a-week treat for me when I'm at home. My job is so busy, I can never be bothered to cook. One good thing about being here is having some free time. I hadn't realised how knackered I was.'

'My job is always knackering, but I don't know any different. My dad's a builder too, and I used to help him out as a kid. I always knew that was what I was going to do.'

'I used to work in the florist's in town on Saturdays when I lived here. I loved it. I went over there the other day, but it's shut down, which is sad.'

'The building's for sale, I think.'

'I wonder what happened to the owner. She was really nice to me. She gave me the painting that's gone missing.'

'Joyce must have moved it,' Adam says.

They eat in silence for a bit. Adam devours his pizza and lets out a satisfied sigh with the last mouthful.

'Thanks for this, just what I needed.'

'Your family must miss you,' Nell says.

Adam pushes the pizza box away and picks up his beer.

'Tell the truth, getting this job has come in pretty handy. The flat we live in isn't very big, and we get on top of each other a lot of the time. Me and Mandy's mum don't get on great, so while I've been here she's been going over more to give Mandy a hand with the kids. When we do see each other, it's better. I know it's only temporary, but…' He finishes his beer and drops the bottle in the recycling crate by the back door. 'Fancy another?'

'I'm fine with this, thanks,' Nell says as he gets another bottle from the fridge. 'Maybe in a bit.' She's enjoying having some company. 'What do you think of Joyce?'

'Joyce is great. I hate cleaning and I wouldn't be able to keep the house how Lilian wants it.'

'Did you know that Lilian's room is locked? But when we had the break-in, it wasn't, because I checked it.'

'Lilian wants it locked.'

'Joyce needs to clean in there. It will get so dusty. Do you know why Lilian doesn't want her to go in there?'

'No idea. It's not my business. I wouldn't worry about it. Joyce does a good job, that's all I care about. She did say one thing, though. She told me I didn't need to worry about trusting her, as she'd worked for Lilian for a long time, and that Lilian said she'll see her right, whatever that means. I reckon she's expecting some kind of handout when the old girl pops off.'

'Yes, she said something similar to me. Apparently she stopped coming for years; do you know anything about that?'

'To be honest, I've not spoken to her much since that first time. You know Lilian doesn't want you asking questions; she made that clear.'

'Leave Lilian to me. I'm going to see her again tomorrow. I'll stop asking questions when she gives me answers.'

CHAPTER TWENTY-NINE

The following afternoon, Nell sets off to visit her grandmother. She decided last night that she'd walk there, worked out the route before she went to sleep, unable to switch off her mind after the conversation with Adam. It's a sunny day, an unexpected bonus, and she's glad of her sunglasses. She inhales great gulps of air as she strides out, hands in her coat pockets. She gets a jolt of pleasure as she passes the bus stop, where a lone man sits. She's feeling so much fitter in the short time she's been here. Who needs fancy London gyms? The membership she took out last year was a stupid waste of money, purchased in the post-Christmas week, another unfulfilled New Year's resolution. She's too tired after work to drag her aching body over to the gym, and weekends are for catching up on sleep. Here she sleeps so much better.

The walk takes forty minutes, during which she mulls over her conversation with Adam. His revelation about Joyce wasn't a surprise. The cleaner hasn't tried to hide her suspicion of Adam's motives, or Nell's own. Does she think they'll try and talk Lilian out of leaving her something in her will? Nell can't imagine asking her grandmother about that sort of thing – it seems vulgar – but as she strides along the country lanes she's contemplating precisely that, her stomach churning at the thought. Could it be Joyce, and not Adam, who wants her out?

*

Lilian is wearing a lilac-coloured shawl over her shoulders, a cameo brooch at the collar of a cream silk shirt.

'You look flushed,' she says, filling the kettle. Nell leaves her outdoor layers by the front door and perches on the sofa in the sitting room, which leads off the kitchen. Lilian's hair is set, not a strand out of place, like a carefully pruned hedge.

'I walked here. It's lovely being back in the countryside.'

'You surprise me. You couldn't wait to escape when you were younger.'

'I'm a different person today. I didn't appreciate what I had back then; I regret that now. All I could think about was my friends living so far away. I was lonely. I'm trying to make up for what I did, though, and I want to get to know you again. I need to know where my roots lie. Surely you can understand that?'

To her surprise, Lilian nods.

'I've been doing a lot of thinking since your arrival. Adopting David wasn't an easy option for me. People talked; you know how this village is. When I discovered I was unable to conceive a child, my life was turned upside down. The world is different nowadays, but back then I was ashamed, and the thought of telling anyone… Joyce found out, which was bad enough. I found it hard to look her in the eye after that.'

'Was that why she stopped working for you?'

'Who told you that?' Lilian's sharp tone surprises Nell.

'She did.'

A look of annoyance distorts Lilian's face.

'She has no right to gossip.'

'Don't blame her, it was me asking her questions.'

'And I've warned you about that too. No good will come of it. And no, that wasn't why she left. That was much later, after the accident. Losing my husband and then my son, I wanted to be alone. Besides, she had her own family to look after.'

'But you weren't alone; you had Sarah and me.'

'Yes, and I've told you how that went. That was another reason I couldn't have Joyce hanging around. I'd made the mistake of confiding in her, and I wasn't about to do it again.'

'She told Adam you'd promised her something in her will.'

Lilian's head shoots up in surprise.

'Joyce says a lot of things; it doesn't make them true.'

Whatever that's supposed to mean, she's dodged the question. Nell shifts in her seat, unwilling to continue with the subject if Lilian doesn't want to talk about it. It feels wrong, and she doesn't want to antagonise her. Not while she's more approachable. It will take time.

'What about my grandparents on my mother's side? You were friends, weren't you? I've found some old photo albums. Why did you never show them to me?'

'Have you been going through my private possessions?'

Nell frowns. 'How else am I supposed to find out about my mother's family? I wasn't to know you were going to start talking.'

'I'll speak to Adam. I don't want you staying in the house if you're going to nose about like that. I'd rather you asked me outright.'

'But I have more right to be there than he does. Surely—'

Lilian holds her hand up, the gesture sending Nell catapulting back through the years, feeling the same burst of fury and impotence the gesture always aroused in her. *Respect your elders*: another of her grandmother's infuriating mantras. But instead of charging out of the door as her younger self would have done, she steadies her breath and considers the best way of framing her questions.

'You said yourself it was important for me to know. Let me ask one more question, please.' She rummages in her bag and takes out the photograph of her four grandparents by the gate. She scans their faces. Gerald is glancing away from the camera as if something has distracted him, and Lilian is holding tightly to his arm, while Charles looks at the camera, looking serious. She holds the photo in front of her grandmother.

Lilian closes her eyes. 'I'm tired now, I have nothing more to say. I've told you all you need to know. Raking up the past is a mistake.'

Nell has been twisting the chain of her locket, which she does now when she's thinking, turning it into a set of worry beads. Lilian opens her eyes and stares at her.

'What's that you're wearing?'

Nell realises her mistake, but she no longer wants secrets between them.

'My mother left it to me. It has her photo in it. The only one I've ever seen of her as an adult.'

She unclasps the chain, then opens the golden heart and looks at her mother. Then her eyes go back to the photograph in her hand and she stiffens, suddenly seeing what her grandmother has been trying to keep from her. Sarah looks exactly like Gerald.

Dear Mary,

It was the photograph that gave me the final proof, and once I'd seen that image, I could never unsee it. The four of us, arms around one another in front of the field gate after one of the many country walks we used to go on. Your daughter Sarah was crouched down in front, a streak of mud on her sleeve. Our faces are flushed in the wind, and we're all smiling, but Gerald is looking slightly off camera, his firm chin jutting upwards like Sarah's, the exact same bone structure visible. The likeness hit me like a bolt of lightning. How could I not have seen it before? Sarah was five years old then, and I crumpled to the floor at the realisation that what Gerald had described as a short fling had elongated into a full-blown relationship in front of my eyes.

It was the photograph that propelled me down to the library that afternoon, where you were opening the new gallery. Was it only yesterday that you'd confided in me how nervous you were about your first public duty as mayor? No need for nerves, Mary, I'd said, but there was now. Armed with the photograph, I marched into town and confronted you, not put off by the ridiculous red cloak and gold frippery that is now your public uniform. As soon as you saw me, you knew what I'd come for. Had you been waiting for this moment for years? It was only afterwards that I realised how many people had witnessed the showdown. Among them a journalist from the local paper, eyes widening with delight at the newsworthy item that unfolded in front of her, pen twitching in her fingers. I didn't mention Sarah, but you knew what it was that had sent me to you like a whirling dervish.

So now you know how it feels to be humiliated in public. How ironic that you have been voted in as mayor – such a poor role model. The powers-that-be must be doubting their choice, but it's too late to do anything; your year in office will have to play out.

The village gossips will be incredulous that we aren't cancelling our holiday together, but it's a perfect opportunity for me. We won't have anything to do with one another once it's over, I'll make sure of that.

Don't worry, Mary, all will be revealed very soon.

Lilian

CHAPTER THIRTY

'Gerald was Sarah's father, wasn't he?'

Lilian closes her eyes. Nell waits. She will wait until she gets the truth.

'Yes,' Lilian says. 'Yes, he was, and now maybe you'll understand why I didn't want David to be involved with your mother.' With surprising strength she snatches the photograph from Sarah's hand. She prods her finger at Mary's face. 'She was my best friend and she did this to me. The only female friend I'd ever had, letting her in slowly over the years, the only person beside Gerald I dared to trust, and she repaid me with this utter betrayal.'

'Did David know?'

She visibly shudders. 'Of course not. My relationship with his father was private, and I wanted to protect him from the truth.' She looks at the photo once more before dropping it on the floor. 'I couldn't believe it when he brought Sarah home. He'd had girlfriends before, but no one serious. I could tell by the way he talked about her that he thought she was special. When he first mentioned her I wasn't concerned as they were only friends at that stage, but as soon as he turned up at the house with her… She was so like Gerald it was torture for me to look at her.'

'I look like her too,' Nell says quietly. Was that why her grandmother was so harsh with her?

'Yes. That didn't help. I prayed for your looks to favour your father, but prayers are rarely answered. I'm surprised David never realised. I wanted to put him off her, but he couldn't understand.

She drove a wedge between us. David assumed I was one of those mothers who think no woman will ever be good enough for their son; he thought marrying her would make me see how serious about her she was, but that only made it worse.

'And what about Gerald, did he know you'd found out?'

'He certainly did. I made it clear to him that he had to cease all relations with Mary immediately. I wrote to her, too, but never sent the letters in the end. It was my way of getting the anger out of my system.'

'I found part of a letter in your possessions.'

'But I destroyed them. I'm sure I did. No good can be done by meddling any further. Please, let this be. I did things I regret.'

'Is that why you paid Sarah's rent? Out of guilt?'

Lilian nods and clasps Nell's hand.

'Leave it,' she whispers, 'please. It won't do any good.'

Her hand feels like the bones of a small bird. Is that kindness Nell sees in her grandmother's eyes? Lilian's fingers squeeze hers. Nell hesitates, then kisses her on her papery cheek.

'You have nothing to worry about,' Lilian says. 'I changed my will as soon as I knew you were back. You're my sole beneficiary. My sister has never liked me; her daughter deserves nothing. Sending her grandson over to butter me up – I saw straight through that. He'll be paid for the work he's done, that's all. But you are my granddaughter, my David's flesh and blood, no matter who your mother was.' She closes her eyes and drops Nell's hand. Nell stiffens.

'That's not why I'm here.'

'I know.' Lilian's voice is a whisper. 'But now you know everything there is to know.'

Nell doesn't for a minute believe that Lilian has told her everything, and she is determined to follow the narrative to its conclusion. On the way home, she walks fast, her mind in turmoil, trying to cast her strait-laced grandmother, such a woman of principle, into this new role of victim.

*

That night she lies in her bed, the story playing out in her head. Rain lashes the windows and she finds the sound comforting. For the first time she imagines herself in her grandmother's shoes, her best friend betraying her in such a way, and wonders how she herself would have reacted. She thinks back to Matt, her boyfriend at university, recalls a Christmas ball where he danced with her closest friend Alice and she couldn't help noticing how they stayed on the dance floor when the music changed to a slower tempo. Was Alice pressing her body against his just too closely, and why wasn't he pulling away? The green flame of jealousy had burned inside her and she'd never quite trusted them together after that. She imagines that feeling magnified. If only she could find the letters. She falls asleep determined to build on the flash of kindness she saw in her grandmother's eyes, and her monumental revelation.

Her mobile wakes her in the middle of the night, an insistent beep. It's bound to be an unsolicited sales call, and she pulls the pillow over her head. Seconds later, the downstairs phone starts ringing. She doesn't want it to wake Adam, so she rushes downstairs and lifts the receiver without speaking. She hears breath, both her own and someone else's, and presses her lips together, determined not to speak.

'I've got the painting,' a gruff voice hisses. It could be male or female. She holds her breath. 'And I'll get you next.'

Her legs weaken and she leans against the wall, hand clamped over the receiver.

When Nell's mobile rings the following morning, she freezes until she sees Jenny's name.

'Hi,' she says.

'I'm on my break at work,' Jenny says, 'so I've only got a minute, but I thought you'd want to know. Gran emailed me, said she'd forgotten to mention that there's a portrait of Mary, and you'll never guess where it is.' Nell can imagine Jenny grinning as she speaks, twirling a ringlet of red hair in her fingers. It falls into place then, the missing piece that's been buzzing in her mind like a bee, the vague familiarity she'd always felt.

'I know what you're going to say. It's the portrait in the entrance hall in the library. I knew it was familiar somehow.'

'Yes! Can you believe it?'

Half an hour later, Nell is standing in front of the painting. The painting of her grandmother. Now that she knows who it is, she can't believe she didn't make the connection. The artist has captured Mary's likeness in bold brushstrokes. The plaque attached to the side of the frame is worn but by peering in close she can just about decipher the inscription: *Mary Henderson, Mayor of Seahurst 1971–72.* She takes a photo of the painting. Jenny comes out while she's staring at it.

'I can't believe I didn't make the connection. When I was younger, I used to come and study here, and this painting spooked me – I always felt like the woman was watching me. She looked familiar, which must be what bothered me. Do you know anything about it?'

'Not a sausage. It's one of those things I pass every day and never pay any attention to.' Jenny steps back to appraise the painting. 'Now you mention it, there is a likeness.'

'Are you due a break soon?' Nell asks. She's desperate to tell Jenny about the phone call in the night. Should she call the police? 'You won't believe what happened earlier.'

'Jenny,' a woman calls out from the library, 'I need you on counter.'

'Coming,' Jenny says. 'I've had all my breaks, but give me a call later. I'm dying to hear your news.'

Nell is on her way to the bus stop when the solicitor rings.

'Good morning, Ms Wetherby. I've spoken to your grand-mother, and can confirm she is perfectly happy with Adam being in the house but regards you as her next of kin. But perhaps you already know this; she mentioned that she's spoken to you. Your return has clarified the situation for her.'

'Yes, that isn't such a surprise to me now. I had a long talk with her yesterday and she told me she has changed her will recently. It was a total shock that she mentioned it.'

'Ah. Obviously I can't comment on the contents of her will, but I can confirm there have been developments in that area. Regarding her current accommodation, she's taken out a six-month rental contract at Sunnydale Lodges, with the option of renewing it if the building work takes longer, but she fully intends to return home once the conversion is complete. But I'm very pleased that relations have improved between you.'

After some pleasantries, he rings off. Ever since seeing Lilian, Nell has been worrying about the new information she's been given. Should she mention Denise being cut out of the will to Adam? In theory she doesn't have to reveal it to anyone, but she's been getting on better with Adam and doesn't want to spoil this. Especially as she has no idea how long she will be staying. The voice of the night-time caller jumps into her mind and the back of her neck prickles with fear.

CHAPTER THIRTY-ONE

The bus journey home passes in a blur. The anonymous phone call is preying on Nell's mind and she's deep in thought as she walks down the drive, vaguely wondering whether Adam will be here, anxiety at entering the house alone slowing her pace. His van isn't in the drive, but a movement at an upstairs window catches her attention and she stops. Her heart beats faster and she rushes to the front door, groping around in her coat pocket for her key. Somebody is in Lilian's room.

But her key isn't there. She rummages in her bag, then empties the contents onto the front doorstep: purse, half-eaten energy bar, pack of tissues, but no keys. Her pulse has sped up, so desperate is she to get in quickly, to catch whoever it is. She pats her jeans pockets, discovering the keys as a bulge in the last one she tries. She leaves her things on the step and her hand shakes as she opens the door, panting, ready to rush upstairs, only to encounter Joyce standing in the hallway dusting the banisters.

'Someone's in Lilian's room.' She tries to catch her breath.

'What?' Joyce glances upstairs.

'Be careful,' Nell says, 'it could be anyone.'

'Why do you think someone is up there? I'm alone here, I haven't heard anything.'

'I saw someone at the window.' Nell grabs a large umbrella from the stand in the hall. 'Stay back.'

She goes up the stairs slowly, listening for sounds. Lilian's door is closed. She pauses outside, then pushes at it, preparing to burst into the room, but meets resistance. She tries the handle. The door is locked. Joyce comes up behind her.

'There's nobody in there, love.'

'There has to be, I saw somebody. Why is it locked?' She bangs on the door. 'Who's in there?'

Silence.

She bangs again, but with less force, feeling foolish. Did she imagine it?'

'Could they have got out of the window?' she asks Joyce, who isn't hiding her disbelief.

'I very much doubt it. It's quite a drop from up here.'

Nell races downstairs and back through the open front door and looks up at the window.

'Nobody's there,' Joyce says. 'Honestly, you're imagining things.'

Nell stoops to bundle everything back into her bag, cheeks burning. What a fool she's made of herself.

'Come inside and I'll make some tea. Your mind's playing tricks on you.'

'I was so convinced,' she says. 'You haven't been in there, have you?'

Joyce laughs. 'If I had a key, I'd have been able to open the room and put your mind at rest. Next time I visit Lilian, I'll insist she gives me one. You've had an eventful few days, haven't you? Seeing your grandmother again after so long, meeting Adam, it's a lot to take in. You're grieving for your mother, that's what's behind all this.'

Joyce prepares the tea and Nell sits at the table. She takes in the large kitchen as if seeing it for the first time. This house will one day be hers. Would she even want to live here given everything that's happened here? Maybe Adam would have appreciated it more. She intertwines her fingers, overcome with embarrassment at her behaviour just now. Joyce sets a mug in front of her, and she wraps her hands round it, welcoming the comforting heat.

'I've been to see Lilian again. She actually talked to me properly, wasn't so secretive. She gave me some unexpected news.'

'Was she telling you about your mother; is that what's upset you?'

Nell nods. 'She told me something that might affect Adam, and I'm not sure whether I should tell him or not.'

Joyce stirs sugar into her tea and takes a mouthful.

'How are you two getting on?'

'Better, that's the thing. We shared a pizza last night and chatted. I don't want to upset him again.'

'You can talk it through with me if that would help. I'm neutral, barely know either of you, but I do know Lilian.'

Nell stares into her cup, as if reading her tea leaves to make her mind up. Joyce is right: she does know Lilian, which gives her the edge over Jenny when it comes to advice. Jenny will be more of an emotional support.

'He talked to me about his family last night. I get the impression they're struggling and he's set his hopes on this house.' She hesitates. 'Lilian told me his mother Denise was down as her next of kin, but she's changed her will since I returned. I can't quite believe it. It's not so much about the house but that she's forgiven me.' Her eyes fill with tears.

Joyce takes her cup over to the sink, although she's only had a mouthful of her tea. 'I've only ever had to deal with one will, which was my husband's; obviously I knew the contents anyway, as we made it together.' She sounds breathless, as if she's having trouble talking. 'I can't bear the thought of Lilian not being around, I've known her for over fifty years.' Now she's drying the mug; this must be how she deals with grief, returning to cleaning, putting things right.

'Why did you stop working for Lilian?' Nell is testing what Lilian has told her. She still sees her grandmother as being slippery with the truth, but hopes she's wrong, that Lilian's words are genuine.

'She wasn't right after the accident. She shut everyone out. It suited me; my children needed me.' Joyce twists her mouth as if she's eating a sour lemon. 'And I'm not convinced she's thinking straight now. This business with the will strikes me as odd. It doesn't mean she won't still leave something to Adam, just that you'll be the main beneficiary.'

'No, that's why I was so shocked. I guess it's up to me whether I want to gift anything to him. She's put me in an impossible position, in fact.' Nell jumps as the cup slips from Joyce's hands.

'Oh my goodness,' she says. 'I'm all over the place. No, leave it, it's my job.' She gets the dustpan and brush from the cupboard and sweeps the china into the pan, her movements fast.

'Joyce,' Nell says. 'Please, sit down. Leave that, it doesn't matter.'

Joyce hesitates before abandoning the dustpan and brush and taking a seat at the table.

'I'm just so upset,' she says, wiping a tear from her eye.

'Of course you are, it's understandable. But just because Lilian is ill doesn't mean she won't get better. I shouldn't have brought up the will. Forgive me for being insensitive; my head's all over the place. I'm not sure I even want the house, to be honest. My mother's necklace is more precious to me than any of this.' Nell gestures around her. 'The reality is, Lilian drove my mother away and I still don't know if I believe her reasons for doing that. She drove me away too. This place holds such difficult memories for me, I can't imagine I'd want to live here. Not that I want Adam to have it necessarily. You're more deserving than he is. I can see how upset you are.'

Joyce's shoulders are so tense she looks as if she might break.

'Why don't you go home,' Nell says. 'You don't need to work, not now.'

Joyce's head snaps up. 'Oh, rub it in, why don't you? I know when I'm not needed.'

'No, I didn't mean it like that.' But Joyce is already unbuttoning her overall. Nell wrings her hands; she didn't mean to upset this woman whose life is so entwined with Lilian's.

Joyce's nod is curt, her movements rapid as she does her coat up. The windows rattle as she slams the front door behind her.

CHAPTER THIRTY-TWO

The evening stretches ahead of Nell. She'd hoped for reassurance from Joyce; instead she's even more ill at ease. She fears Adam's reaction, the news a crack in the glass of their tentative friendship. She makes herself another cup of tea and tries to call Hannah, who doesn't pick up. Too late she realises what day it is; Hannah will be at salsa class without her, followed by drinks in the pub with everyone from the class.

When she hears the crunch of wheels on gravel and sees the lights of Adam's van outside, she checks her hair in the mirror, pinches her cheeks and pulls her mouth into a smile in an attempt to chase the worried look from her face. She sits at the kitchen table and picks up her mug, loosens her shoulders.

The front door slams and Adam stamps his feet on the doormat.

'Hi, Nell,' he says, sticking his head round the door.

'Hi. It looks pretty horrible out there.'

'It is.' He glances at the clock as he comes into the kitchen. 'Christ, is that the time? I've been stuck at the police station for the last hour.' He goes to the sink and pours himself a glass of water.

'What for?'

'They questioned me about my whereabouts during the so-called break-in.'

'I'm glad they're taking it seriously.'

He picks up a leaflet from the worktop and folds it into squares. 'You don't think it was anything to do with me, do you?'

'No, of course not.'

'I was at the hardware store at the time it happened. This job for Lilian is turning into a lot of hassle.'

'It's given you somewhere to live.'

'So that's what you think. Everything was all right until you turned up.'

'You seem angry.'

He starts to tear up the leaflet. 'And I've got good reason to be. I just spoke to Joyce.'

Nell takes a sip from her mug to hide her surprise.

'Interesting conversation we had. Last time I spoke to Lilian, she said she didn't want you in the house; next thing I know she's changing her will in your favour. If I wasn't so mad, I'd laugh about it. Talk about obvious. I suppose you'll be changing the locks next.' He kicks at the pizza boxes, which are stacked by the bin for recycling. 'To think you tried to butter me up with pizza last night. *My treat*, you said. Some fucking treat.' He kicks the boxes harder and Nell clutches her mug to her chest.

'That's not how it is. I went to see Lilian and we talked about me leaving home, and about my mother. I had to mention the will because of what Joyce had been saying to you. I was as surprised as you are when she told me she'd changed it in my favour.'

'I don't believe a word of it. Have you got any witnesses to your conversation? Or were you left alone with her?'

'Be careful what you're implying, Adam. I'm not interested in Lilian's house, or her money. What I came back for—'

'It's obvious what you came back for. Since my grandmother is dead, my mother is Lilian's next of kin; she wanted me to have the house for my family. We need it. You should see our flat, and there's no chance of getting a transfer; we're so far down the council waiting list it's a fucking joke. Lilian hasn't been paying me for the work, that was our agreement.'

'So you want to live in the house?'

Adam looks wary. 'Maybe.'

'That's not what the man in the pub said.'

'What? What man?'

'Gary, I think his name was; he knew Jenny, who I was with. He said you were planning on selling it.'

'What the… Gary Rumbold? What does he know? He's talking bollocks as usual. I hate this town, nosy locals gossiping everywhere you go. What did you tell him about me?'

'Nothing. I'm not interested in gossip either. All I want to know is what happened to my mother.' Adam kicks the table leg, a deliberate thud, over and over, making Nell tense her muscles. 'Please, Adam, try and calm down. Lilian might be winding me up, or you. I still don't know whether I can trust her. She's said some horrible things about my mother. I just want the truth. If the truth is she's giving me this house, I'm not sure I want it. I wasn't happy living here, and my mother was even unhappier by the sound of it.' She pulls the locket out from under her top. 'She left me this when she died, and it means more to me than anything else in the world.'

'I don't think changing the will was Lilian's decision. Besides, I'm a blood relative, whereas your father was adopted, I'm more entitled than you, have to be.'

'Honestly, Adam, this is what she wants. I can only think that seeing me again made her feel guilty about pushing me away. I look so much like my mother, and she couldn't handle that when I was younger.'

Adam goes upstairs and Nell wanders around the house, unable to settle. She won't mention the threatening phone call to him in case he's behind it; she won't show him she's worried. She stares at the empty wall where the painting used to hang and wonders what has happened to it. Was someone in Lilian's room earlier? Or is Joyce right and she's under too much stress? She may have been wrong about the person at the window, but the painting has definitely gone, and nobody has taken responsibility for that.

When Jenny calls later, she seizes her phone as if she's treading water and it's a lifeline.

'Would you like to come over for dinner tomorrow?' she asks. That way she won't have to spend another evening alone in this house with all these weird things happening.

CHAPTER THIRTY-THREE
1994

Sarah stands in the queue at the post office. Her whole body aches and she can barely keep her eyes open. It was such a trying night at work. Somebody had spilt coffee in the corridor; it had splashed down the walls and into the skirting and she had to refill her bucket twice before she could shift the stain completely. Just as she finished her shift, the supervisor appeared and asked her to help empty the bins from the floor below; the weight of them dragged her shoulders out of their sockets and made her arms shake. She wanted to scream at the woman, who's had it in for her ever since she started, and ask her why she couldn't have asked Jerome, who is ten years younger than her and works his muscles at the gym. But she knows the answer: she's seen the supervisor blushing and coquettish with Jerome, and she bit her lip to keep her anger and frustration in as she heaved the rubbish into the bin, gagging at the foul smell.

The queue is barely moving and she yawns into her hand. She finished work an hour ago and should be in bed by now, but she had to wait half an hour for the last night bus. Most of the people in the queue are on their way to work already, smart in their suits and bright-eyed, whereas her skin is grey with fatigue and her shoulders stoop. But she has one pound fifty left in her purse and needs to withdraw some more money before she goes home as the post office is closed this afternoon. The one pound fifty she hands over in exchange for the pack of two spiral-bound notebooks she's buying after the doctor suggested it was a good idea to write down her feelings. She has a lot of feelings, and one book will not be enough.

Back in her kitchen, she counts out the money and works out how much she has left for the week after she has put away the tiny amount she can spare, which she slides into the used envelope in the drawer, resisting the urge to count it. It's nowhere near enough, but it's only a week since her last trip back to Seahurst, her annual pilgrimage. 'Think positive,' the doctor told her, and her last thought before her mind closes down in sleep is how kind his eyes were.

She dreams, as she often does, that she's on a train and is trying to reach her daughter, but the train speeds up each time it gets to the stop where she needs to get out, and she wakes up breathless, her pillow wet with tears. It's been two whole years since she left little Nell; they are virtual strangers. The photo in her locket is the only one she has.

It's late afternoon when she gets herself up and into her dressing gown and sits down at the small table with her notebook. Writing her feelings down will help her while she waits for an appointment with the therapist; so many people have battles to fight just to get through the day, and she kicks herself for taking so long to register with the doctor. It's easy to be anonymous in this big, uncaring city, and when she first arrived here it suited her to wear the cloak of invisibility around her heavy shoulders. It's taken her two years to emerge from the mental fog she's been in, and now she feels ready to start the fight to get her daughter back.

Last week she went back to Seahurst for the second time since she left. The icy wind helped her hide, as she wrapped herself in the thick wool duffel coat she'd found at the charity shop, hood covering her hair and scarf pulled up around her face so that only her eyes showed. She was confident nobody would recognise her, especially as snow was falling and people were concentrating on their feet, anxious lest they slip and fall on the icy pavements. The house was as she remembered it, and she lurked in the bushes outside, grateful for the privacy they offered away from other properties and nosy neighbours.

As she waited for a glimpse of her baby – no longer a baby but a little girl now – she wondered what she looked like, whether her hair had stayed blonde or had darkened like her own into a more anonymous brown. She had to stomp her feet to stop them from freezing. At last the front door opened and a figure emerged. At the sight of the tall figure dressed in black, she bent double, sliced in half by fear the woman provoked in her. She peered over her scarf, watching with greedy eyes as a child dressed in red skipped out and seconds later was bundled into the back of the car. She was grateful she was frozen to the spot and unable to dash over and swoop her little girl up into her arms. Getting her back was going to take time, and she had to be sure of success.

She watched through the clouds her breath made in the cold air as the car backed out of the drive, and tried to imprint the image of her daughter on her mind, gasping aloud as the vision faded and she realised that if she were in a room full of children, she would have no idea which one was hers. She existed, that was the only fact Sarah could take away from today, and she hung on to that as she sat on the train, her limbs thawing and grief flooding through her veins as images from another car in that same drive assaulted her, and a woman sitting opposite offered her a tissue to blot her face with.

Now, here in her kitchen, she writes down everything that has happened since the first time she set eyes on David as an adult. He was standing at the bar in the local pub, sneezing uncontrollably, and she crossed the room, leaving her friend sitting alone, and handed him a pack of tissues from her bag. It had been so many years since she'd last seen him he hadn't recognised her. When he'd stopped sneezing he bought her a drink to say thank you. Her friend went home early, and Sarah and David talked all evening; by the end of the night, they both knew that something special had happened. Her rounded handwriting fills the pages, and she doesn't stop until she gets to the point where she first opened up to the doctor about how she thought she'd been persistently drugged and tricked into leaving her child. It has taken two years, but now she's ready. She is going to get her daughter back, no matter what it takes. She needed to see Lilian once more, to experience that fear again and remind herself of what she is up against.

When she has finally finished, she puts down her pen and sits for a long time. Eventually she gets up and makes herself some scrambled eggs with grated cheese on the top and two slices of buttered toast. She needs to build up her strength, get herself well enough for the fight she has on her hands. She has no money for solicitors, so she can't fight her mother-in-law that way. The only way she can see to get her daughter back is to snatch her and run. And for that she needs careful planning, because she'll only get one chance at it. She owes it to David, and she owes it to herself. She'll make Lilian pay. Of that she is certain.

She'll get her daughter back if it's the last thing she does.

CHAPTER THIRTY-FOUR
2019

Rain batters the windows when Nell wakes the following morning. She'd planned to walk down to the beach, maybe have another swim, before picking up some groceries to cook for Jenny this evening. Adam's car isn't in the drive when she leaves. She can't help looking up at Lilian's window, but today it's covered with raindrops, trickles of water running down the glass. It must have been her imagination yesterday; she's building up a fantasy about a mysterious locked room when the reality will no doubt be more mundane. Lilian always was funny about her room, fierce about her privacy; why change the habit of a lifetime?

She hugs her bag to her chest under her umbrella as she waits for the bus, protecting its precious contents. She's brought Sarah's diary out with her, not wanting to read it in the house. In the village bakery, she buys a coffee and a croissant and takes a seat at the back of the café area. As she eats the flaky croissant, she leafs through a copy of the local paper that has been left for café clients. A picture of the current mayor adorns the front page, and her thoughts turn to Mary. There must be other people apart from Jenny's gran who knew her grandparents, but how would she find them? An ad in the paper perhaps?

A spate of burglaries covers the rest of the front page and she reads with interest. Several houses in the same street have been targeted, and expensive jewellery has been taken from most of them, along with some war medals. Nell wants her own break-in to be related, but deep down she knows her intruder is not after Lilian's jewellery. But what are they after? Could the answer lie behind Lilian's bedroom door?

She returns the paper to the rack and orders another coffee before turning to the diary. She wipes her fingers on a serviette and opens the book. The girlish handwriting makes her catch her breath, as it does every time she opens it.

> I can't believe it's come to this. Yesterday I had to go to the council to find out about signing on. I've worked my whole life, earning just enough to survive, and never have I had to rely on handouts before. I may have little, but I've always had my pride. The grey council buildings dragged my mood down even lower and it was all I could do not to cry.
>
> The lady I saw was kind, but I came away with nothing but leaflets and a lot of muddle in my head. It seems I won't get any money for a few weeks due to changes in the system – she admitted it didn't make sense to her either, so what hope have I got?
>
> I cried then and she asked me if I was in fear of becoming homeless, and I had to explain to her about my rent being paid. But I couldn't tell her I need money for food and travel because I'm looking for Nell. Last time I was in Seahurst the woman in the post office told me that Lilian's granddaughter had left home – for once I was thankful for village gossip. Every week I take the bus and work around different areas of London, looking for my daughter. My biggest fear is having to pawn my locket, or even sell it, if my benefits don't come soon. I'd like Nell to have it one day.
>
> She'll be twenty-six now and I most likely won't recognise her, but I'd never forgive myself for not looking. I

wanted to ask the council lady if she could check on her database, but I knew she'd talk about data protection, and besides, I don't like to think of Nell being in my situation. In my mind she'll have a good career and a loving husband and she'll live in a beautiful house.

Every now and then I read through my earlier diaries; I like to remind myself about the times I went to Willow House looking for her. Every summer for ten years I went there without fail, always during the school holidays, hoping to catch sight of her. When I did see her I'd write down a detailed description, and that's what I read back over now, trying to conjure up her adult face in my mind. It doesn't work, but no matter, I'll never stop looking for her.

My earlier diaries. She knew it. Nell can't read any more. Tears pour down her cheeks and she's grateful for the empty tables around her. She goes to the bathroom and washes her face, gazing in the mirror at the features her mother was so desperate to see. Didn't she know how alike they looked? It breaks her heart to think of Sarah roaming around London searching for her amongst the millions of people who live there. Her shoulders slump at the hopelessness of her mother's mission.

Back at the table, she takes out her phone and calls Moira, her mother's old neighbour.

'Hello?' Moira's cheery voice sings down the phone line. 'Oh, hello, love. How are you getting on with finding out about your mother?'

They chat a little before Nell gets to the reason for her call. 'I'm making slow progress. I've just been reading the notebook you gave me and that's what I wanted to ask you about. There are some missing, you see – she refers to older ones – and I wondered whether she mentioned anything about those to you.'

'Now let me think,' Moira says, and Nell closes her eyes, willing the kind old lady to remember something, anything that will give her a clue. 'I'm afraid not,' she says. 'Apart from the visit that I think led to her giving me that one to look after. It disturbed her, that visit, but that's my reading of it, not what she actually said. She seemed scared that somebody would find it. It would seem strange not to hand them all over if there were others, don't you think?'

'I guess you're right. It's so frustrating.'

'It must be. I wish I could be of more help.'

'No matter, you've been so helpful already.' Nell hears a voice in the background and smiles. Tom, as ever, trying to join in the conversation.

'Excuse me, dear,' Moira says, and her voice becomes muffled for a moment before coming back on the line.

'Sorry about that. Tom has just reminded me that Sarah had a small house fire not long before she died, and was very distressed that she'd lost some books. We assumed she meant novels or something that had special significance for her, but it would make more sense for them to be these diaries, don't you think?'

Nell's stomach plummets. 'I hope it wasn't. I'll never find out then. What caused the fire?'

'An old heater she used in the living room malfunctioned.'

Poor Sarah. As if she didn't have enough to contend with.

It's midday by the time Nell leaves the café. What she's learned this morning has robbed her of her appetite, and she forces herself around the supermarket, picking up ingredients to cook later. While she's paying for the purchases, she's aware of her phone ringing, but waits until she's finished paying before looking to see who it is. Lilian. She deposits her bag on the floor and dials the number, steeling herself for her grandmother's voice.

'Hello.'

'Nell, this is Sandra, your grandmother's carer; we met the other day.'

'Is everything OK?'

'I wondered if you'd heard from your grandmother today?'

'No.' A feeling of unease spreads like a rash across Nell's chest. 'Where is she?'

'I'm sure it's nothing to worry about, but she went out this morning and hasn't been seen since. She does go out most days, but she always lets me know when she'll be back. And she's missed her lunch, which is unusual. I wondered if she might be at her house. She's been a little muddled lately.'

Nell picks up her bag and starts walking in the direction of the bus stop.

'I'm in the village, but I'll go straight back to the house in case she's gone there. I'll call you as soon as I arrive.'

'Like I say, I'm sure there's nothing to worry about, but it's best to be on the safe side.'

'Of course. Thank you for calling.'

Nell thinks back to the recent conversations with her grandmother. She doesn't remember any lapses in memory. When she gets to the house, the landline is ringing and she struggles with her key in the front door, drops her bags to rush in and answer it.

'Hello. Hello?'

Silence, but she senses a presence at the other end.

'Hello?' She slams the receiver down. The house is silent, empty.

She dumps her shopping on the kitchen table and calls Sandra, who promises to let her know if Lilian returns. Next she calls Adam, who doesn't answer, so she leaves a message. The unease swirls in her stomach and grows. What if something has happened to Lilian? What if whoever has been targeting the house is trying to get to her? Is she in danger? Adam calls back and she tells him what's going on. He agrees to drive round to Sunnydale Lodges and talk to Sandra. He tells Nell not to worry until he gets back.

Nell is calmer after speaking to Adam. She chops vegetables for the evening meal to keep herself occupied. She prepares a fish pie and a tray of vegetables to roast and leaves them covered, ready to cook later. By now it's late afternoon, and she texts Jenny and reminds her to come at seven.

She showers and changes into a black shift dress, wanting to make an effort in an attempt to feel better in general. Her black suede moccasins will be perfect, but they aren't where she thought she'd left them. She kneels down to look under the bed; it's spotless down there, and she suspects Joyce has been in despite Nell telling her it wasn't necessary. Something glints, and she pulls out a lipstick that isn't hers; she only brought a neutral one with her, and this is a deep pink, which would look most unflattering on her. It wasn't here when she was burgled, she's sure of that, as she double-checked every inch of her room. Joyce doesn't wear make-up and Adam hasn't been in the house. Or has he? Has he brought his partner here? Or someone else? She turns the lipstick over in her hands as she contemplates where else it could have come from.

The phone rings again. She freezes, alert for the silent caller. But what if it's Sandra? She runs downstairs and snatches up the receiver. Clutching it in her hand, she listens – silence again – then slams it down. She needs a drink. She goes to the kitchen and realises that in her daze earlier she forgot to buy wine. She's wondering whether to go to the local shop when she hears the front door close and Adam calling her name.

'Any news?' she asks.

'She rang Sandra just before I arrived. She'd gone to a friend's, forgot to leave a note. She got quite cross that Sandra had been making a fuss.'

Nell tuts. 'I bet she did. That's a relief. Sandra mentioned she's been a bit forgetful. Perhaps it would be a good idea to organise a check-up for her.'

'As long as she doesn't know about it.'

'Yes. Can you imagine?'

'Something smells good,' Adam says.

'I've invited a friend over for dinner. Jenny, the one from the library, though she's not due for a while yet.'

He hovers in the kitchen, opens the fridge. 'Can we talk? How about a quick drink?' He takes two beers from the fridge. 'Sorry for being moody the other day, but I'd spent ages with the police and I was mad. You might as well know that my alibi didn't check out, that's why they wanted to see me, but I swear on my life I had nothing to do with going through your stuff. I'd asked my colleague to cover for me because I didn't need the hassle, but he had a fit of conscience and went back and told them the truth. Understandably they were even more suspicious, but I think they believe me now.' He drinks some beer. 'And I was pissed off with Lilian about the will because she knows me and Mandy are struggling and she told me I would be all right when she'd gone. I swear she did. But we'll manage, we usually do.'

'Like I said, I'm not sure Lilian is even telling the truth about the will, especially given what Sandra said about her being muddled. Were you here earlier?'

'No. Why?'

'Hold on, I want to show you something, see if you recognise it.' Nell runs upstairs to get the lipstick.

'Is this yours?' she asks, showing it to him.

'Not my colour,' he says.

She rolls her eyes. 'Seriously, have you ever seen it before? Do you know who it belongs to?'

He takes it and winds the lipstick up and down. He shakes his head. 'Mandy only ever wears bright red, and hardly ever since she had the kids. Why?'

'I found it in my bedroom.' She takes it from him and puts it in the kitchen drawer. 'Do you think it's Joyce's?'

He shrugs. 'Could be, I suppose, dropped it when she was cleaning.'

'Maybe. I thought I saw someone in Lilian's room yesterday, but Joyce said she hasn't got a key. Do you know if Lilian has left any of her possessions in there?'

'Not that I know of. But she doesn't exactly confide in me. Apart from telling me the only person Lil ever had any feelings for was David. She worshipped that boy, apparently. Joyce told me she made life very difficult for anyone who tried to take him away from her. Said it wasn't natural, the way she smothered him. Him dying young nearly killed her, so Mum says.'

'Joyce is very loyal to Lilian.'

Adam laughs and drains his beer. 'Well you know why that is. She wasn't best pleased when she heard about the will.'

'She was OK about it, just upset because it made her think about Lilian not being around one day.'

'Good job she doesn't know about her getting forgetful – she might claim she wasn't of sound mind when she made the new will.'

Nell glances at her phone to hide her consternation. That hadn't occurred to her and it concerns her that he's thinking that way. But he'd have heard about it from Sandra anyway. 'I need to run out to the shop before Jenny gets here, buy some wine.'

Adam gets up. 'I'm going out, but I need to finish a job in the shed first,' he says. 'I'll let myself out the back gate when I've finished; I won't disturb you and your mate. I'm glad we had this talk.'

'Me too,' she says. Then, quickly, 'You haven't been making phone calls here, have you? Without speaking?'

For a moment he looks cross, then he grins. 'Heavy breathing? No, not my style.'

He disappears through the back door. Nell's phone lights up with a text from Jenny.

Lots of traffic tonight so I might be a bit late.

But Nell's mind isn't on the text. She didn't mention the heavy breathing to Adam. He's just joking, she tells herself as she hurries towards the shop, but she's not convinced. She still stands between Adam and the house he's been regarding as his own, and despite his earlier friendliness, she's sure he hasn't forgotten that.

CHAPTER THIRTY-FIVE

The bell rings as Nell leaves the shop. The village square is deserted until the local bus trundles into view. A lone woman gets off. Her blue coat and shopping bag look familiar, and as she sets off in the direction of the house, Nell realises with a jolt that it's Joyce.

She speeds up behind the scurrying figure, but Joyce is too far ahead. Perhaps she has left something in the house – Nell can't imagine she's come to clean at this late hour. If she has, she'll ask her to leave. She wants a quiet evening in with Jenny.

She stops off at a bench to sit and watch the sea for a bit; now that Jenny is running late, there's no rush, and hopefully Joyce will have left by the time she gets back. But when she finally gets to the house, she can hear raised voices. Adam must still be around, although he said he wasn't coming back in. She peers through the front-room window but can only make out the glow of the cast-iron lamp that is as old as her grandmother. She lets herself in, then pauses in the entrance hall and listens.

'How could you do this to me?' Joyce's voice is raised and Nell wonders what Adam has done.

'Do what exactly?'

It's not Adam. The voice is female, and Nell reaches to the wall to steady herself when she recognises Lilian's unmistakable tones. Questions race through her mind but she holds herself still, not wanting to alert them to her presence, intrigued at what Joyce is going to say.

Joyce laughs, and the sound gives Nell goose bumps.

'Cut me out of your will.'

Now it's Lilian's turn to laugh. 'What are you talking about?'

'Your granddaughter has been very informative. I wasn't happy about her turning up the other day; it was bad enough having Adam here – all these worms crawling out of the woodwork. Luckily I'm good at pretending, I've put up with you and your moods for years. Talking down to me, acting like the lady of the manor.'

'Why don't you sit down, Joyce, and tell me what it is I'm supposed to have done.'

Nell inches forward to look through a crack in the door. Lilian is sitting in her armchair, Joyce standing by the table. Something is different about her.

'My granddaughter isn't necessarily telling the truth.'

'I wonder where she gets that from.'

'Joyce, please.'

'I went to see your solicitor, you know. Mr Grayling. Asked him about your will. He wouldn't tell me anything, of course, but I saw the pity in his eyes. I told him all about your great-nephew and granddaughter turning up, both so blatantly after your money. I wouldn't be surprised if they've known each other for ages, just put on this charade for my sake, to get the better of me. At least I've been able to warn Mr Grayling. If you tell me I'm wrong, then of course I'll go back and put him straight. Because you promised me, didn't you, Lilian? You promised me you'd see me right. Don't you remember, all those years ago, when you sent me away, asked me to keep my mouth shut? I even let you get away with telling poor Sarah that I'd taken her money. Don't look so surprised. She told me why she was so upset, and I put two and two together. I know how your devious mind works. But I kept my mouth shut, I haven't said a word to Nell, although she's bombarded me with questions. Persistent she is, like an annoying little dog yapping at my heels. Maybe you were trying to shut her up too? Is that what this is? You told her you'd changed your will just to shut her up?'

'My will has nothing to do with you.'

Nell's left leg has developed cramp and she's desperate to move it but terrified of alerting them to her presence. She wants to know what Lilian has to say as much as Joyce does. Already she's reeling at seeing this side of Joyce. And then it strikes her: Joyce is wearing make-up; the pink lipstick is what's different about her. Of course. How could Nell have thought it was Adam trying to frighten her off when all along it was Joyce?

'Oh, but it does. Have you forgotten what I know? I've kept that secret for over twenty years. Nell would love to hear what really happened to her grandparents.'

Nell bites down hard on her lip to stop herself from gasping aloud, mesmerised by the sight of Joyce through the crack in the door. Jenny could arrive at any moment, and she hopes the traffic is still bad – she doesn't want anything to stop this conversation. What does Joyce mean about her grandparents?

'I plan to tell her myself.'

Joyce grips hold of the back of the chair in front of her. 'You can't, you won't. She'd report you and you'd go to prison.'

'I'm old and I've got cancer. What do I care about going to prison? I can see right through you, Joyce. If I tell her and everything is out in the open, you won't be able to blackmail me any more, will you.' Nell hears a squeaking sound as Lilian eases herself out of the armchair. Joyce stands up straight and takes a step backwards. Nell holds her breath as if she's a spectator at the theatre, the old lamp in the corner throwing a spotlight on Joyce.

'Rubbish. Why would you go to the bother of trying to frighten her off? All those phone calls, the break-in, the graffiti – I didn't think you'd got the energy.'

Lilian's face turns white. 'How do you know about that?'

'I saw you letting yourself in on more than one occasion. Nothing gets past me. Why did you try and frighten her?'

'Because I didn't want her here. She's my granddaughter, she's David's child, and I love her. Opening up all this business about her mother is only going to cause her grief. I was trying to protect her from the truth. She doesn't need to know what I'm capable of. And you'd do well to remember that yourself, Joyce.'

Joyce stiffens. 'It's true then, isn't it? You were responsible for David's accident. I always wondered but didn't think even you would go that far.'

'I never meant to harm him.' The words burst from Lilian like air from a balloon and it's all Nell can do to stop herself from gasping. 'That woman was plotting to take him away from me; she'd got a house lined up and everything.' The veins in her neck are standing out as the words spill from her. 'She was meant to be driving that evening. A little tampering with the car, that was all it would take; she was like poison ivy trailing around my house and I had to get rid of her. She could have stopped him; I ran after the car as it drove away and she pretended not to see me, forcing my boy to drive to his death.'

'And yet you still blamed her.' Joyce shakes her head slowly. 'That poor woman lost her whole world in a few seconds.'

'She survived.' Spittle bursts from Lilian's mouth and Nell can barely cope with the horror of what she is hearing, covering her mouth with hands that are shaking uncontrollably.

Lilian is moving closer to Joyce as she speaks and can't see that Joyce is reaching to her side, towards the lamp on the table. With one swift movement she grabs hold of the lamp and swings it. Nell screams and rushes into the room, bashing her hip against the door in her haste. Lilian's eyes widen as she catches sight of her.

A loud smash makes Nell jump, and Lilian slumps to the floor. Blood pools around her head and glass lies broken beside her. Nell drops to her knees beside her grandmother, oblivious to the shards of glass that dig into her.

'Are you hurt?'

'What are you doing here?' Surprise erases the look of pain on Lilian's face. 'Did you hear…' The sentence trails off as she screws her face up in pain.

'I heard everything. You killed my father, destroyed my mother's life after failing to kill her, and ruined my childhood. And you've been tormenting me ever since my return.'

'I was trying to protect you.'

'At what price?' Nell fixes her eyes on her grandmother's and sees them dim. Lilian gasps and her body contorts, then she goes limp.

'Lilian?' Nell suppresses a scream. Now she knows the truth of what Lilian has done, she doesn't want her to escape retribution. But Lilian's eyes are fixed on the ceiling, devoid of life, her mouth slightly open.

'What have you done?' Nell looks up at Joyce. She sees Adam in the doorway, but not the lamp that crashes down on her own head.

CHAPTER THIRTY-SIX

When Nell opens her eyes, Adam is leaning over her. She screams and tries to fight him off, but the movement makes her head throb.

'Shush, stay calm,' a female voice says. Jenny is kneeling next to her. 'You're safe, it's OK.'

Adam's face swims into view again. 'No, keep him away,' Nell says, and he disappears. She grabs Jenny's arm. 'Ouch, my head hurts.' Pain surges, and she can hear a banging noise.

'It's OK,' Jenny says, stroking her hair out of her eyes. 'It could have been a lot worse. It wasn't Adam. He's on your side; he saved you from that crazy woman.'

'Joyce.' Nell feels a stab of fear. The lamp is on the floor, but there's no sign of the cleaner. The slash of pink lipstick and the eyes full of hate flash back into her head. She digs her fingers into Jenny's arm, scared to let go.

'It's OK, she can't hurt you now.'

'But Adam can.' She tries to push herself up onto her elbows, but a wave of nausea makes her drop back to the floor. Jenny doesn't realise the danger she's in.

'He's on your side, Nell, trust me. He forgot something and came back, heard a commotion and saw Joyce was about to attack you. He managed to grab her arm but couldn't stop her hitting you completely, just with less force. He says she would have killed you. That lamp is lethal.'

Nell recalls her grandmother's glassy eyes and her teeth begin to chatter. 'Lilian is dead, isn't she? Joyce killed her. She's dangerous.

Jenny, where is she now?' Her voice is getting shrill and Jenny strokes her forehead.

'In the next room. Adam's restrained her. The police and ambulance are on their way. I'm sorry I was so late. There was a burst water main in town; the police were redirecting traffic and it took ages.'

The banging noise intensifies.

'What's that?'

'It's Joyce. Adam has locked her in the kitchen. Do you know why she did this?'

The sound of a siren drowns out Jenny's words and she goes to the door. Two policemen come in, followed by two paramedics; one checks Lilian over before shaking his head, while the other attends to Nell, and one police officer goes into the kitchen while the other speaks to Jenny. Moments later, Joyce is led out of the house in handcuffs. Adam hovers in the doorway.

'We need to take you to hospital,' the paramedic tells Nell.

'My head's a bit better now,' she says.

'You've had a head injury, so you need to be checked over.'

'I'll come with you,' Jenny says.

Jenny holds Nell's hand in the back of the ambulance. The hospital is only a ten-minute drive away, but the journey seems to take forever. Her grandmother killed her father, wanted to kill her mother, then severed her from Nell, and she squeezes Jenny's hand to combat the pain this knowledge brings. *I was trying to protect you.* Lilian's justification for her actions has no meaning to Nell.

'The pain relief should kick in soon,' Jenny says, but Nell knows this pain will never be relieved. The loss of her grandmother is wedged like a blade through her heart.

CHAPTER THIRTY-SEVEN
2018

Sarah trudges home, her feet hard to lift, as if she's wearing heavy boots, the pain in her head like she's never felt before. She didn't even protest when she was given the news. It had been coming, she'd known that, as inevitable as the darkness that is descending as she makes her weary way home. Pride stopped her talking to her manager, letting him know the situation; if she'd done that, maybe he'd have given her a chance.

He'd sent a message via her team supervisor, asking to see her when she'd finished her shift. Her whole body had tingled with anxiety. She'd had one room left to clean at that point and she did her best, but the hoover was so heavy to cart around and she felt dizzy every time she bent down. She scrubbed at a persistent stain on the floor, her knee sore where she leaned on the bone. She risked taking another painkiller, even though she'd had two before her shift, as her head felt as if it would burst open. She used to fly round this corridor, leaving behind spotless rooms and gleaming floors, but now, with the pain stabbing behind her eyes, it was impossible. The stain wouldn't shift completely, and she still had to wipe the tables down, dust the whiteboard and projector and make sure all the equipment was where it should be. These college lecturers didn't hesitate to complain if the room wasn't left to their liking. She kept her eye on the clock and made sure she wasn't late to go up and see Mr Dean.

The cleaning supervisor's office was little more than a cupboard, but it didn't stop him pulling rank. His wide girth and vast expanse of stomach just about fitted behind the desk, which was covered with paper and half-drunk cups of tea. A man of plenty, where she had little. The small sink was full of plates and cups waiting to be washed. The room smelled of tomato soup. He waved a hand at the wonky wooden chair opposite him and she sat down, clutching her keys in her lap. She still wore her work uniform; she'd have to get changed after this, meaning she'd be home even later than usual. She was thankful he wasn't going to offer her a drink, because she couldn't bear to use any of the crockery. She might not have much, but she had her pride, and cleanliness was the one thing she could control. Her flat was immaculate, as her offices used to be before all this started.

She rubbed her forehead, willing the pain to ease off for a moment. The strip light in the room was intense and it hurt her to look up.

'Do you know why I've asked you here?'

She shook her head, and her stomach clenched.

'You used to be one of my best workers, Sarah, but you know that because we talked about it before, didn't we, at our last meeting, when I had to give you a verbal warning.' He sighed. 'I don't like having to do this, you know. Is there anything I should know about? Anything that would go in your favour? I understand you're a private person, like to keep to yourself, but if there's anything we can do, this is your chance to tell me about it.'

Sarah pressed her lips tightly together, hands clutched in her lap. She imagined for a moment telling him about the headaches, but that would require hospital visits, prescriptions she can't afford, time off work, and it would get her a bad reputation. She'd had it drummed into her when she was in school that absenteeism was a bad thing, and she'd seen it here too. Polly, who'd worked on Level 3, was dismissed after taking time off for depression. It was all very well saying mental health was important and should be taken seriously, but in practice everyone knew employers didn't like it. She'd got on with Polly, was sorry to see her go; Polly had even given her her number, but there was no point calling her as she had no spare cash to do anything social anyway, and she'd thrown it in the bin.

Mr Dean shook his head. 'You aren't making this easy for me.' Sarah didn't think it was her job to do that. He stared at her for a moment. 'Fine. Your work isn't up to standard.' He swiped on his iPad and passed it over to her. 'These photos have been taken of your work over the last few months. Look, it's unacceptable. This floor looks as if it hasn't been hoovered in weeks, and there are coffee stains on the wall. This is your last chance to give me an explanation.'

Sarah looked fleetingly up at him and then back down at her lap. His eyes were kind, but she remained silent.

'All right. You know the procedure. You've had your written warning and there's been no improvement in your work, so you've given me no option but to dismiss you. You'll receive your pay as normal at the end of the month, but you need to leave your uniform and security pass and anything that belongs to the college, and take all your personal effects from the building. I'm sorry, Sarah, I really am. You've been a good worker for a long time but I can't sustain this level of incompetence.'

Incompetence. The word sounded over and over in Sarah's head as she went back to her locker and cleared it out. She packed her work shoes and her jumper and gathered up some old payslips; not much to show for over twenty years working here. She doubted anyone would notice she'd gone.

By the time she gets home, her head is pounding and she feels hot, so hot. Another letter lies on the doormat, accusatory, with the hospital logo on the back. If hospitals did red warning letters, this would be one. She's been unable to attend any of the previous appointments due to her work commitments, but now she'll be free to go. Her doctor will be pleased; she's been persistent, reminding her, rebooking the missed scan, only for her to miss it again. But what would be the point?

She discards the letter without opening it and goes straight to bed, pulling on her warm pyjamas and getting under the duvet. Lights are flashing behind her eyes and she buries her throbbing head in the pillow, curls in on herself like an embryo. She strokes the gold locket around her neck; it usually calms her down, but today it does nothing for her feverish head.

The pain is too severe to sleep through and she's taken as many painkillers as she dares. In her febrile state she's unable to stop the memories assaulting her. It's like a needle is stuck in the groove of a record, scratching over and over but unable to make any headway. She'd had such high hopes when she finally confronted her mother-in-law; she had her lines prepared and her arguments polished. She was Nell's mother and she was determined. But it didn't go to plan at all.

Now that she has lost her job, the one thing in her life she'd managed to hang on to, what reason does she have for carrying on? Her head throbs and the fever burns and she succumbs to it, not caring whether she ever wakes up again.

Dear Mary,

I'm writing this on the veranda of our Spanish villa, the sun beating down on Torremolinos, the heat showing no sign of abating though it's past six o'clock in the evening. The still water in the pool waits for someone to disturb it with a graceful dive or a reckless jump, but it will remain calm as I am the only occupant of the villa this evening, my hair still damp from my shower after an interminable afternoon at the beach. All traces of sand have been removed and a gin and tonic with large chunks of ice sits in front of me.

You'll have noticed how I've been sticking to my husband like a leech, Mary, so my announcement this evening that I was suffering from sunstroke and not up to going out will no doubt have surprised you; don't think I didn't see the glimmer of hope in your eye. But your soirée out together is all part of my plan. Charles will be with you, of course, so the most you'll be able to manage with my husband is a whispered word, an indiscreet touch perhaps, but it's my way of testing Gerald, because I will know when he returns tonight whether anything more has happened between you. I will see it in the way he moves and behaves, and in the words he says as we prepare for bed, alert for that particular tone he uses when he's lying. Let's hope for your sake he is blameless, because any whispered words will have consequences and you will come off worst. But then you must already know that.

I don't think Charles suspects anything, poor hapless man; he always was a bit wet, the last to grasp the meaning of a joke, to formulate a witty response. Unlike *my* husband. I'm impressed by the way you've played your part. An outsider would never know there was any discord between us, like the street photographer yesterday who took such a good photo of our group that each couple bought a copy. *Each couple.* Whatever that means now you've blurred the boundaries of who belongs to who. We've laughed over jugs of sangria and tapped our feet and smiled at one another as the young Spaniard plays flamenco guitar and the crickets chirrup in the background, unmistakably foreign sounds, a world away from the wet Seahurst evenings.

I wish I'd been there when Gerald told you I knew about your sordid secret. Was he kind to you, or was he brutal, dismissing you with a telephone conversation perhaps? That's the scenario I like to imagine when I go over it in my mind, adding more details with each retelling. A cold tone on the telephone, frost travelling along the line, making you shiver inside. It's what you deserve, Mary, you must know that.

I expect you'll be relieved when this week of enforced togetherness under the Spanish sun is over. You'll be happy for the tan to fade and will attempt to erase this trip from your memory. I've noticed you haven't taken any photographs yet; so unlike you. Take a few, otherwise even slow-witted Charles might notice and wonder. He might begin to question whether it's the heat that's making you thrash around in the bed at night, rather than the anguish of your split from Gerald and the guilt at the way you've betrayed me.

But there's no need to worry; your agony is about to come to an end. Not on the flight home, which looms ever closer; only forty-eight hours to go now. Oh no, it won't be that easy. I've got something special planned for you, something rather spectacular.

Not long to go now, Mary. You'd better make the most of this evening out with the two men you have made fools of. It might never happen again.

Lilian

CHAPTER THIRTY-EIGHT
2019

Nell stands outside Willow House. Behind the shuttered windows the building contains the horrors of her family history, and she wants rid of it. There isn't a shred of doubt in her mind. The FOR SALE sign went up yesterday.

Last weekend she travelled back to London and went out for dinner with Stacey. By the end of the evening Stacey understood why she was handing in her notice and starting a new phase of her life.

Sarah's funeral is held separately from Lilian's, a quiet affair, attended by only a handful of people. Mr Grayling and Hannah's father sorted out all the arrangements, giving Nell time to grieve.

Mr Grayling is confident the estate agent will sell the house quickly; they're asking a good price. Nell plans to give Adam a lump sum from the proceeds, so that he can sort out his family situation. He's down on his luck, like her mother was, and she can give him the chance Sarah never had. The rest is enough to buy herself a flat near the coast; back by the sea, where she belongs. She's got an appointment with Fairfield and Evans next week, not only to find somewhere to live, but also to view the old florist's shop where she used to work. *Go for it!* Hannah said. *It's meant to be.* She'd love to surround herself with colour and beautiful fragrances and give pleasure to people every day. She's ready for a slower pace of life and a different focus.

Nell puts down the last letter and picks up the now familiar photograph. Four friends on holiday, sunshine, palm trees. It's what's hidden that interests her. The secrets behind the smiles plastered on for the camera. The relationships that tie them together with invisible strings. How many times has she pored over this photograph, wondering what is eluding her?

Now that she knows the whole story, the missing piece is as dazzling as the sun in the Spanish sky shining down on these four people. What is significant is that Lilian and Gerald were on the Spanish holiday with Mary and Charles, a fact omitted in the article about the accident. Knowing the influence Lilian had, she wonders if she put pressure on the journalist to keep the information out. She knows now that not only did Lilian drive her mother away, she also killed her father and her grandparents. But despite everything, Nell survived the accident, and through her, Sarah lives on. She holds the locket close to her chest and thinks about her mother, hoping wherever she is she is making her proud.

CHAPTER THIRTY-NINE

My days are limited on this earth; there is nothing left to fight for. My granddaughter is determined to find out the truth, despite my attempts to drive her from the house, and I need to write this all down, to clarify events in my mind before I draw my final breath. I owe her that much.

I could have asked Adam to fetch the letters from my bedroom and bring them over to Sunnydale, but I no longer trust him. I never sent them to Mary in the end. I ventured to the post box several times but couldn't bring myself to do it. I valued my freedom too much; once I'd carried out my plan, questions would be asked, and I had Nell to think about after all. I've asked the solicitor to give them to her after I'm gone.

Nell. How Sarah failed me by giving birth to a girl. I'd convinced myself it was a boy, a boy carved in his likeness, a boy to replace my David, whom Sarah had taken away from me.

The girl looks so like her mother.

I wanted to love her.

I hope she can forgive me.

Dear Mary,

You won't be reading this letter, but it's therapeutic to write it all down. Or maybe you are; I like to think there's some kind of afterlife, that you can hear me talking to you. I talk to you a lot, Mary. I like to imagine your face as I'm telling you my story. I'll set the scene for you. I'm wearing black, of course; it's only been a week since we got back from Spain, and I'm in mourning: two of my close friends have died, after all. I must act the part. Poor Charles was unlucky to get caught up in this and I am sad for that. Gerald has been busy at work all week, his way of dealing with it – he doesn't want me to see his grief-stricken face and I don't mind. He'll get over it.

The postman brought me a surprise this morning. Remember the photograph we had taken in the street, the four of us? I'd forgotten I'd placed an order. In this photo we didn't have our arms around one another as in so many earlier ones, but we were all smiling. Gerald's smile looked genuine, though it's hard to know how he was feeling; we never did discuss our feelings. His face was angled off camera again – he obviously thinks that side of his face is favourable – but it reminded me of the photo by the gate, and the treachery it revealed that sent me flying into town to confront you. Sometimes I'm reckless. I'm working on it.

There was nothing reckless about what happened in Spain. Did you wonder, in those moments when it happened, Charles cursing when the brakes failed to work, his foot pumping uselessly against the pedal? Did your life flash before you and did you know this was no accident? Did you realise the significance of my smile when I waved you off; did you see me kiss Gerald; did you wonder if it was for your benefit?

It was.

Now let's move forward in time, Mary; you'll want to know what happened after, or perhaps you are watching down on me from above – I like to imagine you can see what I do. You'll want to know what happened to David. Even all these years later a shard of glass pierces my heart every time I think of my poor boy. Doctors have prescribed painkillers and mind-altering drugs over the years, but I have a pile of the little green prescription slips in a drawer – medication won't take this away from me, although they came in handy when I needed to add to Sarah's medication, and as for talking therapy, I'd rather throw myself under the 11.05 express to London. Writing therapy is the only route I have, and it no longer matters who reads it, as soon I will have passed on.

A therapist would see through me, you see, the way I've convinced myself over the years that it was Sarah's fault; that she was the one who stole my boy from me and tried to blacken his heart against me. My baby boy who from the moment we saw him in the orphanage squeezed his little fists around my heart and never let go.

After the unfortunate Spanish holiday, Gerald and I didn't mention you and Charles again and devoted all our attention to David. My boy never wanted for anything. He went to the best fee-paying school in the district and excelled in all subjects. I wasn't thrilled when he got a girlfriend – no woman could be good enough for my boy – and when he told me he was bringing her home to meet us, I was nervous but did my best to be as welcoming as possible. I'd share him with the right woman. Imagine my shock when he turned up with Sarah.

How was I to know she would have grown up to be such a beautiful woman? She remembered us vaguely, of course; she was young back then and had been through a lot. Gerald's face didn't give anything away although he must have known. I knew instantly, of course. I couldn't even pretend to like her. She had to be got rid of immediately. Even though David was adopted, Gerald was his adopted father and Sarah's father. It was all wrong.

But Sarah had her mother's tenacity. She took hold of my David and wouldn't let go. Just like you had with Gerald. He'd never been mine again, not really, not in the old, loving way. I don't think he realised how I caused the accident, how I tampered with the brakes of the rental car, laughed and smiled as you and Charles went out for a spin around the winding coast. He had wanted to go with you but didn't dare question my insistence that he stay with me. He had to experience the consequences along with me.

Seeing Sarah holding David's hand with her slight fingers and precisely manicured nails made me dig my own worn nails into my palms. I felt a stirring of the old resolution I'd had all those years ago. Some things cannot be allowed to happen.

A different car from a different time flashed through my mind as I stood in the doorway of my home to wave Sarah off. David turning up, a conversation through the half-open car window, Sarah shifting across to the passenger seat, the realisation at what was about to happen, David folding his long body into the driver's seat. The scream in my throat as I ran out, too late, cursing the length of the drive that enabled David to accelerate – always one to drive too fast, I'd told him so many times and he never listened – such thoughts in my head as I hurtled after them. Too late. She saw me, Sarah, pretended not to, thinking she'd triumphed. The car disappeared from sight, the car I'd tampered with in the way that had worked so perfectly in Spain.

And Sarah survived. I'll make her pay for that look, Mary. If only you were here to watch me.

A LETTER FROM LESLEY

Dear Reader,

I want to say a huge thank you for choosing to read *I Know You Lied*. If you enjoyed it, and want to keep up to date with all my latest releases, just sign up at the following link. Your email address will never be shared and you can unsubscribe at any time.

www.bookouture.com/lesley-sanderson

As with my first three books, *The Orchid Girls*, *The Woman at 46 Heath Street* and *The Leaving Party*, I hoped to create an evocative novel about obsession, secrets and the blurred lines between love and lies. Family relationships lie at the heart of this novel, which gives plenty of scope for drama.

I hope you loved *I Know You Lied*; if you did, I would be very grateful if you could write a review. I'd love to hear what you think, and it makes such a difference helping new readers to discover one of my books for the first time.

I love hearing from my readers – you can get in touch on my Facebook page, through Twitter, Instagram or my website.

Thanks,
Lesley Sanderson

        www.lesleysanderson.com

        lsandersonbooks

        @LSandersonbooks

        @lesleysandersonauthor

ACKNOWLEDGEMENTS

So many people have helped me along the way with *I Know You Lied.*

Thanks to the lovely people of the Lucy Cavendish Fiction Prize for short-listing me for the 2017 prize, for the kindness of everyone involved with the event and their continued support.

To my lovely agent and Bookseller Rising Star of 2019 Hayley Steed, and to everyone else at the fabulous Madeleine Milburn agency for their ongoing support. Hayley, your belief in me means the world, and I love your energy and enthusiasm.

To the Next Chapter Girls – Louise Beere, Clêr Lewis and Katie Godman – you know how much you and this writing group mean to me. I couldn't have done it without your belief in me and my writing.

To my lovely editor Therese Keating – it's been great working with you for the first time on this book. I hope there will be many more to come. To everyone at Bookouture, especially Alex, Kim and Noelle, who does my fabulous publicity – you all work tirelessly and with infectious enthusiasm for your authors and I'm so proud to be one of them.

And to everyone else – all the other writers I've met along the way, too many to name but nonetheless important – I'm so happy to be one of such a friendly group of people.

To my family, to my friends old and new for believing in me, I daren't name you in case I miss anyone out, but thank you.

And most of all to Paul, supporting me all the way.

Printed in Great Britain
by Amazon